"Why is everyone staring at us?" Because moment we had entered the station. I could feel their eyes following us up the stairs.

"Don't know." Logan's shoulders were slightly hunched, and he'd shoved his hands into his jacket pockets. "Not enjoying it."

"Me neither." I looked over the railing, and some people remembered they had jobs to do. Others continued staring. "It's creeping me out."

An explanation came at the landing, where Stannett stood brandishing a copy of the *Santo Trueno Daily*. "My condolences. You're famous."

Discord Jones

A Little Street Magic

Gayla Drummond

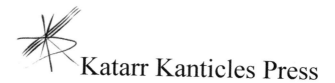
Katarr Kanticles Press

This is a work of fiction. Names, characters, places and incidents either are the products of the author's imagination or used fictitiously, and any resemblance to actual persons, living or dead, business establishments, events, or locales is entirely coincidental.

Katarr Kanticles Press
Texas, USA
Edited by Tonya Cannariato
Copyright © 2014 Gayla Drummond
Cover by Gayla Drummond

ISBN-13: 978-0692634103 (Katarr Kanticles Press)
ISBN-10: 069263410X

Acknowledgments

Super big thanks to you, the reader!
Without you, this series wouldn't have happened.

A Little Street Magic

ONE

The water was the exact temperature to ensure relaxation, and I felt completely boneless as I floated. Moira's hand cupping the back of my neck kept me in the center of the small pool, and grounded me in the here and now. She was murmuring an appeal to the ancestors, asking for them to appear to us.

Not that I was in trouble. It was Sunday, January 6, 2008—a Red Letter day because it was the first Sunday I'd managed to spend with the clan since my adoption ceremony. It had been a good day, filled with fun, food, and plenty of cuddling—mostly with Logan.

I'd finally had the time to discuss seeing the tiger ancestors with the red-haired shamaness. I'd seen them three times: at my adoption ceremony, during a dream in the Unseelie realm, and again at the Solstice bonfire a couple of weeks before. When Moira said she knew of a way to try to discover what had happened to the White Queen who'd helped me locate Logan, I was all for trying.

It'd been a little weird, getting naked with another woman, especially one I knew had been naked with the guy I was dating. But she was the clan's shamaness, and she said the nudity was necessary. She also assured me no one would come peeking.

We were in a circular cave, the pool smack dab in the middle of its floor. The cave was somewhere in the forest behind Moira's cute log cabin. If I opened my eyes, I wouldn't see anything but swirling steam—or maybe it was fog—high overhead. Considering we hadn't descended any great distance, and there hadn't been a huge hill aboveground, the cave was a weird place. Then again, that was kind of par for the course when it came to pocket realms.

Moira paused, then quietly said, "Open your eyes and tell me what you see."

It took a few seconds to obey, because even my eyelids were relaxed to the point of not wanting to move. Once opened, I managed to focus and said, "The ancestors are up there, but they're sitting this time."

"Good. You see the empty place?"

"Yes." The spectral tigers sat in concentric rings, each bigger than the one inside it. All of them that I could see were staring down at us. "It's in the inner circle."

"That innermost circle is the First Clan," Moira said. "The clan that all others are descended from. Which means that the missing White Queen is Cerridwen."

Not an English name. Irish? But there weren't tigers in Ireland. Not native ones anyway. I could ask about that later. Bigger fish to fry at the moment. "What do we do now?"

"We'll ask her mate where she is. Remember, they're spirits, and our ancestors."

"Yeah, but they're not my ancestors. I'm adopted."

Moira softly chuckled. "They approved your inclusion. They accepted you as one of us."

I wanted to ask them why, but maybe it was better not to know. Didn't really want to learn anything that might ruin my newfound joy in belonging to the clan. "Which one is he?"

There were ten other tigers in that innermost circle, nine oranges, and one black. I knew the black tiger wouldn't be the missing Queen's mate, because black tigers were sterile. He was nearly solid black, having only a few, subtle pale markings. He sat on one side of the empty spot.

"Matthew," the shamaness called, and the orange tiger on the empty spot's other side blinked large, pale gold eyes. She began to greet him, so I took the time to look at the rings of tigers.

There were more circles than I'd first thought, receding into the outer limits of visibility of the cave's foggy ceiling. I spotted over a dozen White Queens in the circles I could clearly see, some with black striping, others with brown, orange, or gold striping. There were only three black tigers in those circles. From the one in the First Clan circle to the third in the fourteenth circle, the last I could easily make out, their markings became more noticeable.

A movement refocused my attention directly above us, and I watched Matthew climbing down invisible rocks. He was gazing intently at me. "What's he doing?"

"Telling us where Cerridwen is. It's all right." Moira lifted her free hand from the water to touch my arm. I'd relaxed into a starfish shape, arms out, legs apart. Nice and vulnerable. Easy prey for a tiger to rip to shreds.

"Everything is fine," she said. "He won't hurt you."

Logan trusted her, and I didn't have any reason not to trust her as well. Matthew reached us then, and sat beside me, across from Moira. The tiger stayed above the water's surface, as though it were solid ground for him. He lowered his head, and I met his eyes.

They were calm and steady. Being that close, I could see the light yellow and green mix that made up the pale gold. The tiger nodded once, and laid a huge front paw on my chest. It was a weird sensation, not any actual pressure, but I definitely knew he was touching me. "She's stuck inside me. That's what he's saying, right?"

"Her spirit's within you, but whether or not she's trapped there is the new question." Moira let her hand slip away from my arm. "He's staying calm. That's a good sign."

"Does that mean she's okay?"

"This is unfamiliar ground for me, Cordi. Matthew knows her location, and isn't angry. He's not upset at all, which I can only interpret as she's choosing to be where she is, and is fine."

The tiger blinked, lifting his paw while looking from me to Moira. His mouth began opening and closing slightly. "What's he doing?"

"He's calling to his Queen. Maybe he can retrieve her."

"Okay." A weird sliding, wiggling sensation occurred inside me. I couldn't tell if it was in my mind or a real sensation somewhere in my body. "I just felt something."

"Painful?"

"No, weird." The strange sensation continued, and my body began to tingle. "Now everything's beginning to tingle."

Moira's hand slid over my bicep again, and her fingers were trembling. Her voice was steady and calm. "Tell me exactly what you're feeling."

"Tingling all over, like my whole body is regaining blood flow. And a," I hesitated, trying to find just the right description for that sliding, wiggly feeling. "Oh, I know. You know how cats sometimes do the Twist on the floor, on their backs? It's like there's a cat inside, doing that."

She smiled. "That's good."

"It is?"

"Yes because it means she's not in distress. I'd guess it also means she's not trapped."

Well, that was a relief. The White Queen was alive, and not stuck. Or whatever passed for "alive" when it came to spirits. "Then she should be able to leave, right?"

"Right. When she's ready. Helping you locate Logan apparently wasn't her only reason to do this."

Matthew quit his silent calling, dropping his head to press his muzzle to the side of my face. He gave my forehead a single lick and turned to begin climbing thin air back to his place in the ancestral circle. I wondered if he'd gotten more solid or something, because I'd felt the caress of fur and the roughness of his tongue instead of vague sensory reactions.

"Guessing he's okay with the situation."

The shamaness nodded. "Looks that way."

We watched him reach his spot, and Matthew silently roared. All the tigers stood up, and began to pace. Their rings slowly condensed into the single circle of tigers I'd originally seen, and after a few more moments, the tiger merry-go-round faded into the fog and out of sight.

"Wow."

"That was interesting. I'm sorry I wasn't more help."

I grinned at Moira. "Are you kidding? We know she's in one piece and seems to be okay. That's awesome."

My cell phone chose that moment to play the opening bars of "Bells, Books, and Candles", Damian's ringtone. Grin fading, I sighed. "Ugh. Duty's calling."

"Sorry about this."

Logan glanced at me, his eyes crinkling at the corners as he fought a smile. "I've never seen you this relaxed. Not even when you were asleep. It's nice."

"I can barely walk." My whole body felt rubbery, and my joints weren't cooperating.

Moira had had to help me, from leaving the pool and answering the phone, to drying off, getting dressed, and returning to the main building.

He'd taken over from there, half-carrying me to his car. We'd left Dane behind to enjoy the rest of the evening with the clan.

"It'll wear off; enjoy it while it lasts."

How did he know that? "Done some soaking yourself?"

"Yeah, it's a good tension reliever."

"Yup." I was not going to ask if he'd been there with Moira. We were officially dating, but we weren't sleeping together. It wasn't my business if he'd had a nude soak with her. Shifters got naked around each other all the time. It didn't mean... I pulled my thoughts up short, aware of Logan glancing at me again.

"Something wrong?"

"Nope." Nothing but my stupid, unnecessary jealousy.

He braked for a stoplight. "You sure?"

"Uh huh. Damien said it's a messy scene. Advance warning: I'm probably going to puke."

"That's why you wanted a bottle of water."

"Yeah."

Logan changed the subject. "Did you two find out anything?"

There hadn't been time to talk about that before leaving. "Yes, we did. She's still inside me, and seems to be okay. Her name's Cerridwen. She's..."

He interrupted, turning wide eyes my way. "The First Queen? That Cerridwen?"

I nodded. "The light's green."

"Oh." Logan turned back to face the road and let off the brake. "The First Queen's spirit is inside you."

"Crazy, huh?"

"Mind-blowing. I can't believe I'm important enough that the First Queen would be moved to help you find me."

Why wouldn't he think he was important enough? "Well, now you know you are."

"And she's still here."

"Yeah, and why is the big question."

He shook his head, shot a quick look at my face, and signaled for a turn. "I'm not sure how to feel about that."

"Makes two of us."

"It was weird you could see the ancestors, not being a shifter. Now it's beyond weird that one has set up shop in you. And not just any ancestor, but her."

I moved around enough to look at him. "My life has been weird from the second the Melding began. As weird goes, this is on the 'Cool Weird' list."

"The 'Cool Weird' list?"

"Yeah, it's the list of stuff that's not trying to kill me."

He laughed. "What's the other list?"

"It's the 'Not Cool Weird' list." I shrugged. "I'm not always original when it comes to naming lists."

"I think it does the job. We're almost there." Logan hesitated. "Do you feel different?"

"I don't think so. She's been in me for nearly a month now. Didn't know she was there for sure, until tonight. It did feel strange when she moved."

"She moved?"

We could see the flashing red and blue lights now. "Tell you about it after we're done here, if you want coffee later?"

"Sure." He frowned. "There's a crowd."

"Ugh."

TWO

I'd never figured out why crowds gathered at crime scenes. Especially one on a late Sunday evening, on a street of business buildings, all of which had been closed for hours, if not all day.

Yet there were a few dozen gawkers crowded around the three strips of yellow crime scene tape stretching out from a shop front. Pettigrew's Curiosity Shoppe, read the sign over the door in a decorative, old-fashioned script.

The three uniformed officers watching the line weren't there just to make certain no one crossed. They were also studying faces, because some criminals got a kick out of sticking around the scenes of their crime.

A few feet from the crowd of onlookers, I stopped. Logan checked his next step, head turning and one eyebrow rising. "What?"

I kept my voice low. "I'm going to eavesdrop."

He nodded and shoved his hands into the pockets of his jacket. The air was chilly enough that I wished I'd thought to bring my gloves. Since I hadn't, I followed suit and found a peppermint in one pocket of my dark blue pea coat. Then I closed my eyes.

My telepathic ability was one of those that was always on. I'd first learned to mute the noise of other people's thoughts to a dull, tolerable buzz in the back of my mind. Thanks to a suggestion from my fairy godfather, Sal—who was actually a real god—I'd recently learned to quiet the buzz even more. I'd built a maze in my mind, and had given each ability I was aware of its own room.

Since it was my maze, I could take the straight route to open those imaginary doors, but I was beginning to practice visualizing the process. Some of my abilities were pretty scary, so it was my way of increasing my control over them. Once I opened the door, I could hear whispers. I allowed them to grow stronger.

Poor old man. He was so nice.

Wonder if the building will be up for sale soon?

I scowled at the back of the blonde head that thought had come out of. "And they say women are the gentler sex."

"What?" Logan edged closer.

"Nothing important." I went back to listening. Yup, people were awful. Most of them wanted to see a little gore to liven up their dull lives. They wanted to be able to tell others "I was there. I saw it."

If that's what they wanted, they should spend time in the Barrows before the vampire carnival closed down.

None of them were thinking guilty thoughts, or satisfied, murderous ones. I sighed and visualized closing the door to my telepathy's room. "It was worth a shot. Let's go."

We excused ourselves through the crowd until we were at the yellow tape. I dug out my license for the cop. "Discord Jones. Detective Herde called me in."

"Yeah. Who's he?"

Logan produced his wallet, showing his license. I introduced him. "Logan Sayer, one of my partners."

"He didn't mention two were coming. Hang on." The cop used his phone to send a text, instead of the mic attached to his uniformed shoulder.

"I could've done that."

He shrugged. "Beat you to it."

We put our licenses away. A man a few feet down the line was staring at me. Too intently for my comfort, but all the other gawkers were curious about us as well. A ding signaled the reply on the cop's cell.

"Okay, you're both cleared to enter. Someone will meet you just inside the door."

"Thanks." I ducked under the tape as he lifted it, and hurried across the sidewalk to the shop's door with Logan a step behind. A bell hanging on the door announced our arrival, and as it shut, Schumacher shoved a box of rubber gloves under my nose.

"Put these on. Got some cute little booties to go over your shoes too."

"Oh, I've been fine," I said, picking out two gloves.

He rolled his eyes. "Yeah, same here. Wish we weren't always meeting at places like this though."

I began pulling the gloves on. "That bad?"

"Did you bring a barf bag?" He put the box on a shelf after Logan took a pair. "You're going to need it."

"No." The last bit of my rubbery, warm relaxation tucked tail and crawled away whimpering. I looked around, noting the shelves seemed to hold junk, not anything curious. "Man, and it's been such a great day."

"Welcome to my life." Schumacher grunted, holding out another box. "Booties, kids. It was a back entry job, so no one goes behind the counter without them."

I checked the aisle we were on, and saw the waist-high swinging door blocking the break between two glass-fronted counters at its end. About five feet past it, a black curtain hung inside the framed edges of a doorway. "Why did I answer my phone?"

"You're an idiot?" Schumacher finally cracked a weary grin. "I answered mine too."

"I'm about to add to my nightmare collection, aren't I?"

Logan said, "I'll sit up with you, if you can't sleep tonight."

"Remember you said that." Shoe coverings in hand, I trudged down the aisle, hoping I didn't end up vomiting on something important.

"There's a wastebasket with a clean liner right behind the counter. It's on the left. I even threw in some paper towels for you," Schumacher said.

"You're too good to me."

"Only the best for my favorite societal menace."

He wasn't following us. I stopped and looked back. "You're not coming?"

"Up close and personal once was enough for me, thanks. I'll be sticking to the photos." The burly detective waved us on. "Don't forget your vomit bucket."

Turning around, I hesitated, so not wanting to walk through the curtained doorway. But since I kind of had to, in order to be of assistance, I started walking again. Logan followed suit, and we paused to put the shoe coverings on before going through the swinging door.

He grabbed the wastebasket and handed it to me. "Here you go."

"Water?"

He pulled the bottle from inside his jacket. "Got it."

This close, even with the curtain, I could smell the tang of blood in the rather musty air. I flipped my hair over my shoulders and hugged the little wastebasket to my chest. "Here we go."

Logan nodded and pulled the curtain aside. Two men standing directly beyond it stepped apart and turned to look at us.

I saw the thing dangling at the end of the rope, felt my forehead wrinkle for puzzled second, and then realized the thing had once been a human.

Chunk blowing promptly followed.

"Better?" Logan finished wiping my face. I was sitting on the floor behind the counters, after coming close to passing out from the violence of my vomiting.

"Not really." My face was burning with embarrassment, thanks to being laughed at by the newest member of the detective division, one Frank Dodson.

Dodson was seven feet tall and solid as a mountain, with pale blue eyes and light brown hair cut in a close buzz. No one looks good throwing up, but none of Santo Trueno's finest had ever laughed at my weak stomach before.

Damian had come damn close to punching the much larger man before Schumacher had intervened and said something that shut down Dodson's roaring hilarity.

"Want some water?" Logan offered the open bottle. I couldn't even meet his eyes, though he'd spent a good ten minutes wiping away pressure induced tears and streamers of drooling vomit.

Accepting the bottle, I took a mouthful to swish around, and winced at the tiny leftovers it loosened. I spat the water out, wiped my mouth with a paper towel, and swallowed a much smaller sip. My throat burned, and my entire torso hurt. The stink of puke was plastered in my nasal passages. At least, I hoped it was just the smell.

It had been that kind of pukefest.

"Cordi."

I forced myself to look up and meet Damian's eyes. My warlock friend smiled. "Can you try again?"

"Considering the volcano of vomit she spewed, she should be dry for a year." Dodson snorted. He sounded like a horse. "Thought she was supposed to be a badass."

Damian's smile disappeared, and he aimed a narrow-eyed glare upward, being a foot shorter than Dodson. "You're going to step back now."

"Or what?"

"Or I call Stannett and tell him the new guy's a jerkoff," Schumacher said from behind the counter I was sitting against. "Then again, Jones could complain. It's not like that was professional behavior, Detective."

I could do that? Hm. I took another sip of water, letting its coolness soothe my throat.

Dodson lumbered out of the counter area, muttering "Bunch of losers" as he went.

"Maybe we should think of creating a chart," Logan said. "Because that is not what I'd call 'messy' in there."

"Hey, I tried to warn her. Did you really say 'messy'?" Schumacher asked.

Damian grimaced, but didn't get the chance to reply because Dodson broke in. "Do you people do any actual work? Or do you sit around scenes, playing nurse to the delicate little psychic?"

Logan stood up, looking over the counter. "She doesn't like seeing the aftermath of people being killed. That's not delicate, it's human."

"You didn't spew your dinner everywhere."

"I'm not human."

Dodson sniffed. "So seeing a torn apart body doesn't bother you?"

"It bothers me. Doesn't seem to bother you much though. You laughed." Logan's voice had developed that soft, scary tone.

Which meant the testosterone level was rising too fast for comfort. I quickly climbed to my feet before Dodson could reply, and said, "I'm ready to take another look."

All four men looked at me, and disappointment flashed across Damian's face. Suspicious, I 'pathed him, *Do you want Logan to beat him up?*

Well...kind of.

And get arrested for assaulting an officer of the law?

He had the grace to look embarrassed.

Argh. Fricking men. I stomped over to the curtain. "Logan, come on."

My summons put a halt to the stare off he'd begun having with Dodson. He joined me at the curtain, where I took a deep breath and lowered my eyes to the floor before pulling the material aside. The floor was bad enough, splattered with blood and bits of...stuff. Yeah, "stuff" worked for me.

I picked a way through it to a clear spot behind a big wooden crate to the right of the doorway, Logan following. He was sniffing the air. I breathed through my mouth, hoping not to smell anything. Damian stayed just inside the doorway.

"You smell anything weird?" I asked.

Logan wrinkled his nose. "Blood and cooked meat."

Ugh. Why did I ask? "Not magic?"

He shook his head. "Sorry."

"I guess that's good, or we might have more bodies."

"Victim's name is Arthur Pettigrew. Seventy-three, white male, owner of this shop. Body was discovered by one Brian Fogbottom, who'd arranged to meet the vic at eight." Damian paused. "Pettigrew is a widower, lived alone except possibly for his dog. I'm sending men over to his house."

"How do you know he has a dog?"

Damian pointed to a desk on the other side of the doorway. "Photo."

"Oh." I frowned at the top of the crate, thinking about the junk out on the shelves. "Why would anyone meet a junk dealer by appointment?"

"He wasn't just a junk dealer. He dealt with antiques and other specialty items."

"Special? Do you mean stolen?"

"No proof of that at this time. Fogbottom had a request in for a first edition book. Ah, *The Happy Prince and Other Tales*. It's by..."

"Oscar Wilde," Logan said. "Haven't read it myself, but I did see a copy at the library last week. Guessing not a first edition."

"Probably not," Damian agreed. "First edition for it runs around forty thousand, and I don't think the library has that kind of budget."

I peeked at the body, or what was left of it, and my stomach clenched in protest. "I don't think book collectors do that to people."

"Depends on the book." Logan was studying the hanging body. "Someone hunting down grimoires might have the power to do that."

I dropped my eyes back to the crate's top, noticed there was a bit of finger bone with blackened skin attached, and closed my eyes. "That is now duking it out with old Henry Wilkins for worst thing I've ever seen."

"Wilkins." Damian snapped his fingers. "The serial killer who skinned his victims alive. From now on, anything this bad is a Wilkins."

"Noted." Logan was sniffing again. "I don't understand how there's so much blood."

"It always looks like too much for one person." I opened my eyes, wanting to close them again immediately. Instead, I studied the late Arthur Pettigrew's hanging remains.

His head, most of his chest, and part of one arm had survived the explosion. Everything else, ka-blooey all over the room. There were streaks of rawness showing through the blackened exterior.

"Not what I meant." Logan pointed under the body, and to a few other spots where blood had spilled. "That's fresh blood. Or rather, not boiled blood. It landed there before the perp blew him apart."

"Perp?"

"Guess I've been reading too many thrillers lately."

"I mean, perp works, I just prefer bad guy or killer myself."

"Perp is correct," Damian said. "I hate to ask, but can you pick up any scents that would indicate a vampire or shifter did this?"

I shook my head while Logan did more sniffing. "Wouldn't be a shifter. They can't do magic, so would've had to use actual fire and an explosive. Did anyone hear a boom?"

"No vampire scents, but the blood and meat smell is pretty overpowering. Not much smoke either. I'd kind of expect more."

I side-eyed Logan. "Have you smelled burned people before?"

"No, but I burned a roast and the smoke filled up my apartment."

"A person isn't a roast, Logan."

"We're all meat to someone." He nodded at the remains. "That poor old guy was definitely meat to whoever killed him."

I hated when people made points like that. It did bad things to my worldview. "That's not a cheerful idea. Hey, Damian."

"Yes?"

"Why don't you do that past time-lapse spell?"

The warlock rolled his eyes. "Look around. I can't draw a clean circle in here. By the time this place is fully processed and then cleaned, it'll be too late for that spell to work."

Foiled. "Why isn't anything easy anymore?"

No one bothered to try answering. Damian decided to theorize. "Two possible motives leap out. Either someone had an issue with our vic, or he surprised a thief, who turned violent."

There were open boxes on the shelves and a few crates on the floor. One of the crates was opened. "Is there a safe?"

"Over on this side, and torn open. Can't tell if anything's missing, but if robbery was the motive, the perp wasn't interested in money. There's a few cash stacks in the safe."

"Has the safe been done?" was my next question.

"Only the door and interior edges. Everything's been photographed, but the contents haven't been dusted yet."

"Okay." I began to pick a path to the other side of the door. Damian sighed. "Cordi."

"What?"

"Everything's been photographed and your shoes are protected. You don't have to mince."

"Mince?"

Logan backed him up. "You're mincing. Definitely mincing."

"Fine. I'll keep right on mincing, because I don't want to step on little bits of Mr. Pettigrew. That's disrespectful." Also extremely disgusting, shoe coverings or not. Crap, I shouldn't have thought about that. I'd probably have a nightmare about tiny Pettigrew pieces crawling all over me now.

The safe was a solid box with a keypad and handle. I didn't envy the person who had to process the contents, because they were as gory as everything else. What the hell had gone on in this room?

As I crouched down, Damian came to stand behind me. The handle of the safe was bent out nearly straight, and the bolt was wrenched out of shape too. "Wow, the killer has to be super strong. Is this bolted to the floor or wall?"

"No, and it wasn't moved. It's still right against the wall."

The top was dusty and free of handprints. "So what? He just yanked the door open really fast?"

"Don't know."

Right, that's why I was here, to try and shed some light. "Glove coming off."

"Just the handle," Damian reminded me.

"I know." I touched the handle and waited. After a moment, I let go. "Nothing useful, sorry. Just a sense of satisfaction. Business kind, not 'Ah-ha, I killed a guy' kind."

"Damn."

I stood up and Damian turned to look at the remains.

"Dude, I'm not touching that."

"I didn't ask you to."

"You thought it really loud, and I'm standing right here."

"Idle thought. You couldn't until the autopsy's done."

"Not touching it then either." Uh-uh, no way, no how.

Damian grunted. "How hot does a fire have to be to cause a human body to partially explode like that?"

"Fire doesn't explode bodies, at least not by itself. It cooks the moisture out, burning from the outside in." Logan cocked his head when we looked at him. "I cut open my roast to see if the center was edible."

"Again with the roast." I pointed at him. "We're going to have a talk about mentioning food at murder scenes, mister."

"Sorry, but my observation stands. The outer layers were completely dry and blackened, the inner portion dry and brown. It didn't explode, it shrank." He looked at the remains too. "There's still raw flesh on that part. But all the pieces are burnt."

My stomach began to roil again. Right. "Unless you have something else I can try psychometry on right now, I need fresh air."

"No, but come into the station tomorrow. I should have some things you can handle then."

"Sure."

"Sorry for ruining your evening."

I glanced at Pettigrew Partial. "It's nowhere as ruined as his was."

We started for the door, and I asked, "What's going to happen to his dog?"

THREE

I sat on the floor, my eyes locked to those of a silent Rottweiler. An animal control officer had hold of the dog, with a pole and loop. Tilting my head, I checked the tags hanging from his collar. "Rufus, huh? You're lucky the cop you bit is a dog lover, or he may have fed you a bullet for dinner."

Rufus stared back impassively.

I straightened my head. "My name's Cordi, Rufus, and I can understand you. I'm afraid I have some bad news."

Rufus kept staring.

"Mr. Pettigrew was killed at his shop. If you'll talk to me, you might be able to help us find out who did it."

More staring. The AC officer was shaking his head. "You do know dogs can't talk, right? I'd like to go home, lady."

"For your information, I'm a psychic, and dogs do talk. Remember that the next time you're putting some down. They're probably begging for their lives." Satisfied by the sick expression appearing on his face, I turned my attention back to Rufus. "Come on, boy. Talk to me."

The Rottweiler continued to stare. I moved a little, but his eyes didn't follow me.

"I need help."

"You damn sure do," The AC officer muttered.

I ignored him, and called for backup. "Leglin."

The pole hit the carpeted floor as the AC officer backed away when my hound appeared. Rufus didn't move.

"What the hell?"

I ignored the man. "Leglin, this is Rufus. He lost his master tonight. I can't get him to talk to me."

Leglin stretched his nose toward the other dog. "*Hello, Rufus.*"

No response. My hound sniffed the dog's muzzle, and licked his cheek. Rufus, kept staring, a black and tan statue.

"*He's in shock,*" Leglin said.

"Crap. Get me that blanket."

The AC officer shook his head. "You know what? You're on your own, lady. I'm out of here."

"Fine. Get that thing off him."

"I'm not getting anywhere near that monster of yours."

"He won't hurt you, and he's not a monster. He's an elf hound. But whatever." I scooted forward and removed the loop from Rufus. "There. Leglin, the blanket, please."

The AC officer picked up the pole and held it between him and Leglin as he began to edge past. My hound looked at him, and softly growled. "*He smells of death.*"

"Not surprised. He works at the pound. They put animals to sleep there. Permanent sleep."

Leglin growled again, louder. The guy went pale, and suddenly bolted.

"That was just plain mean," Logan said from the doorway. "All he does is his job."

"He won't be doing it on Rufus. Besides, you've never been to the pound. It's awful. They put dogs and cats down after 3 days, and all the animals know it. I could tell that before I learned to actually talk to dogs." Leglin brought me the blanket. I wrapped it around Rufus and moved to sit beside him. After putting my arm around him, I said, "You're not going there."

"Where is he going?"

"To see a vet if he doesn't snap out of his shock soon. He may know something. Even if he doesn't, I'm not going to let him end up at the pound. People don't adopt dogs like him much. Bad press. Not as bad as pit bulls get, but," I shrugged. "I'll take him home. For now."

Logan smiled. "I knew you were going to say that the minute we got here and saw him."

Rufus shuddered and blinked. I hugged him. "Hey, I'm Cordi. That's Logan, and this is Leglin."

He let out a heart-breaking whine. "*Master is gone.*"

"I know. I'm sorry. But I'm going to take care of you."

Logan pulled out his cell phone. "I'll call Damian."

I left the doggy huddle, accepting a cup of coffee from Logan when I reached the kitchen. "He doesn't know anything. Pettigrew was a nice old man, never gave any sign he was having any problems."

"How's Rufus doing?"

"A little better. That's helping." I nodded at the dog pile. Bone and Diablo were cleaning the Rottweiler's face and ears. "I'm glad you asked Damian about his stuff."

"Familiar things help people. Figured it would help him." Logan took a drink of his coffee. "Are you going to keep him?"

"I don't know. Kind of have a full house, and the Tinies aren't happy I brought a big stranger home." I'd had to shut them in the guest bedroom.

"Sunny might take him."

"No. She found homes for her little guys. Doesn't want another dog living there, except Kyra." Kyra was Tonya's Husky. "Kyra goes to the shop with Tonya now."

"Oh. What about your dad?"

"Maybe. Depends on Betty and Amadeus. You saw how he freaked out over my Pit Crew." I had a drink. "But two little boys may be the right medicine."

"If your dad can't take him, I'll give him a try. Or Terra might. She misses Romeo, that German Shepherd from the dog fighting group. Took forever to find his owners."

"Okay. If the Tinies come around though, I'll keep him. Let's give it a week, see how things shake out."

Logan nodded. "We probably shouldn't talk about the case where he can hear us."

"No. I kind of don't want to talk about it at all. Except Dodson. He was a prick. I can't believe Stannett hired him." I took another sip and leaned against the counter.

"I don't think his coworkers think much of him."

"Damian wanted you to whomp him."

Logan chuckled. "The thought crossed my mind, but you didn't seem keen on that idea."

"I've never had to bail someone out of jail. I'd like to keep it that way."

"I promise to do my best not to end up in jail." He nodded at the dining area. "You were going to tell me about your visit with the ancestors."

"Right." I led the way to the table, and proceeded to do so, ending with "I guess we should find out why she's staying. But I also want to know why an ancient tiger shifter has an Irish name."

"Cerridwen's Welsh, not Irish."

I made a face. "Okay, but tigers aren't native to Britain, so my question stands. Did you know she was a normal tiger first?" Thorandryll had explained to me why the elves treated shifters like second, no, fourth-class citizens.

Logan looked down at his empty coffee cup and fidgeted with its handle. "Cerridwen wasn't the first shifter. Her brother was, or at least that's what our legends say."

"So he learned to change shape, and taught her?"

"Not exactly."

I folded my arms and rested them on the table. "Usually, when I have questions and you have the answers, you pop them out. What gives?"

He sighed and leaned back, keeping his eyes on his cup. "We're the youngest species, maybe around three and a half thousand years old. Before then, we were... just animals. Elves and humans both hunted us, sometimes to capture. Our legends say that Cerridwen and Berian, her brother, were captured by elves. One of their princes was enamored with a human woman, and he gave the tigers to her as a token of affection, hoping to win her hand."

"But she wasn't human," I said. "Right? You said elves have a history of abducting humans. If she'd been human, he would've just kidnapped her."

Logan nodded. "She was a mage from one of the great families. Elves are arrogant, but not to the point of going to war with the children of the gods. Especially not back then, when the gods were actively involving themselves in everything."

"Wait a minute. Didn't any of the gods pick an elf to have a baby with?"

A quirk of his lips said "no" before he answered. "The gods apparently preferred humans."

"Ooh, bet that went over like a fart in church."

Logan laughed. "Haven't heard that one before, but yeah. Anyway, he gave them to her as a gift, and she must've been a child of Cernunnos or some other god associated with animals, because she was able to tame them."

"They became devoted to her, and never left her side. She probably named them." He hesitated. "This is where the legends diverge. One says Berian loved his mistress and grew jealous of the elf and others who wanted to make her theirs. The other says she could change forms, and taught him how to. Both legends agree that she and Berian loved each other, so I guess it doesn't matter if he learned to change his shape by force of will, or if she used magic to teach him to change shape."

"I think it's more romantic if he did it, but if he did, how did he teach the others to do it? And who is the 'she'? You haven't said her name."

"Because no one speaks her name. I know it sounds like a great love story, but it's not. It's a tragedy."

"Crap, I'm not going to like the rest, huh?"

"Sorry."

I sighed. "Go ahead."

"Whichever way it went, the animals of the other mages were affected too. First Berian, then his sister, and after them, the ability to change shape spread to a pair of wolves kept by another mage of her family. It kept going, until every great family's wild pets were able to take human shape."

"The mages liked it, but I'm guessing no one else did."

"Right, especially the elves and some gods. Elves began hunting and killing shifters, trying to stop the spread. Someone decided that since Berian was the first to change, he was the source, and if he died, the others would lose the ability."

Even though I'd been warned the story ended in tragedy, I was fascinated. "What happened to him?"

"They ran, but back then, there wasn't any escape. Everywhere they went, word would eventually spread, and the elves would come. Berian decided to sacrifice himself for her, their child, and his sister." Logan frowned. "But she didn't want him to."

"She called upon the gods of her house to save them, and made a deal. Her life for theirs and all the other shifters. I guess she made a good argument, but there were conditions made. The first groups— Clan, Pride, Pack, and so on—were declared off limits for hunting, but their children weren't protected once they reached adulthood."

"The other condition was that all shifters would be forced to return to their animal shapes every full moon." Logan looked me in the eyes. "I may have lied to you about something."

"What?"

"I told you black tigers were sterile, and no one knew why. Berian was a black tiger."

My heart felt funny, as I remembered the silent black tiger sitting beside Cerridwen's empty place. "Oh. You said they had a kid."

He nodded. "One child. The thing is, one rumor says he was sterile and she worked a spell to allow them to have the child. But there's also rumors that either a god or the elves cursed Berian with infertility, and any tiger that resembled him with the same, as punishment for being the first shifter."

"Well, if no one knows which rumor is truth, you weren't lying about it. That's what you told me: No one knows why," I said, relieved.

"I've always thought the curse rumor was true. Just seems most likely, considering she chose Berian, and elves have a reputation for jealousy. So do gods, and an animal learning to change shapes, or a mage daring to push the envelope, would be stepping on their toes." Logan fidgeted with his cup again, turning it in circles.

"Yeah, sounds about right. But just because you think that's the reason doesn't mean it absolutely is. Quit feeling guilty. Not telling your choice of 'why?' isn't the same as lying."

He nodded. "Cerridwen may know."

I sat back, struck by his quiet tone. This was serious, and the only reason it would be serious to him was if he really wanted kids. And I was a hundred percent certain I didn't. Big problem since we were dating. Huge problem, since I thought I was well on my way to actually being in love with him. "She's not talking to me."

"I know. But if she does... "

Crap. "I'll ask her."

"Thank you." Logan looked up for a second. I hoped my expression wasn't weird. "It's late. Are you going to stay up?"

"No, I think I'll try and sleep." I needed alone time more than worrying about potential nightmares.

When he looked up again, meeting my eyes, it felt as though a wall slid between us. "I'll take Speck and Squishy home for the night, if you want me to. They're awake and still fussing about Rufus."

I couldn't hear them, but I didn't have shifter hearing. "That would be great. Maybe you could keep them for a couple of days, give him time to adjust?"

"Sure. Terra won't mind puppy-sitting while we're working."

We traded smiles, but something had definitely changed between us, and I didn't like it.

FOUR

"Cranky" didn't begin to describe my mood after my alarm clock went off on Monday morning.

It was cold, Bone and Diablo were obnoxiously bouncy, and I couldn't remember if I'd had a nightmare or not. Maybe I was mad at myself for letting personal stuff overshadow Mr. Pettigrew's horrible end.

I'd seen a lot of gruesome things over the past few years, thanks to my psychometry and retro-cognition abilities. Plus more than a few events I'd been personally present for. Never in a million years could my younger, pre-Melding self have imagined that she'd grow up to become a private detective, much less a psychic one.

The dogs, Rufus included, spread out as I began jogging, to sniff for interesting spots to pee on.

I tried to remember, without success, if I'd told Logan that I didn't want kids, when we'd had our heart-to-heart in the Unseelie realm. If I hadn't, he'd probably figured it out last night due to my less-than-enthusiastic agreement to ask Cerridwen about the black tiger sterility thing.

My abilities had already painted a huge bullseye on my closest friends and family, with two having paid the ultimate price and two more having endured terror that was still playing havoc with their mental well-being. I missed Ginger.

It wasn't as though I lacked good friends, but none of us had grown up together. Ginger had been my "sister from another mister" as the saying went. Yet she was gone, and if Derrick were correct, she was at peace.

I was really glad none of my abilities involved communicating with actual ghosts. There were hundreds, maybe even thousands, of psychic abilities. Everyone kept pointing out that I had a lot, and compared to what I'd heard about most psychics, I did. But my dozen or so abilities weren't even the tip of the psychic iceberg.

To be honest, I wasn't even certain I had a couple of those abilities. Not once had I been able to consciously create the protective shield. For that matter, I could only remember one instance of a precognitive vision coming true.

And if those two weren't new abilities I had, that meant someone else was involved. My list of who that could be was short. In fact, it only had one name on it: Sal.

The cold air wasn't responsible for the chill coursing down my spine. Logan had been awed to think he was important enough for an ancestral spirit to decide to help save him. I didn't like the idea of being important enough to have a god interested in me.

Or two. Sal hadn't been alone, using me as a pony ride into the Unseelie realm.

Dried and frozen grass crunched underfoot. We'd reached the first back corner, so I slowed to a walk. I hated being important enough to some people that they wanted to bring me to heel, knowing that a few of them, or maybe even all of them, weren't above threatening my family or friends to get their way.

My fifteen-year-old self hadn't had to worry about this kind of crap. I blew out a deep huff of air, and watching the white cloud that resulted dissipate, said, "I have got to do better."

There hadn't been anyone to really teach me when I woke from my coma. Alleryn, disguised as Dr. Allen, had helped me learn a few things about controlling my abilities. But elves weren't psychics, or natural mages. They were elves, and their magic was different. They could speak a few words, or create potions and such to do what they wanted.

From the first, my learning had been piecemeal. Frankly, I hadn't gotten out of that rut. I'd been reactive, instead of proactive. That had to change. I had to stop waiting to learn stuff until it became a matter of life and death.

Also, I needed to do a much better job of organizing my life so I could spend time with the people I'd added to it. Last night shouldn't have been my first Sunday gathering with the clan. It shouldn't have been yet another crime scene meeting with Schumacher.

Having reached the other back corner, I broke into a jog again, the dogs bounding ahead of me. I'd done a lot of stumbling into alliances and because of that, was now "Somebody" in the supe world. It was time for Discord Jones to grow up, stop sulking over the lost portion of her life, and quit being a clueless dumb-ass masquerading as a do-gooder.

I could do better, and I was going to, damn it.

Sudden barking made me look up from my feet, missing a tangle of weeds and nearly kissing the ground. About a dozen yards ahead, the dogs were lunging into the evergreen bushes, their barks translating to "*Intruder!*"

I caught my balance and ran forward. "No biting!"

They harried a man out of the bushes, who did trip and fall, practically at my feet as I reached them. "Who are you, and what the hell are you doing trespassing on my property?"

"Call off your dogs. I'll sue if they attack me." He rolled over, revealing pale blue eyes that were a match for Thorandryll's in iciness, and a cold-reddened nose. "I mean it."

"Sit." Leglin and Rufus obeyed faster than Bone and Diablo, but all four did mind. The last thing I needed to be rushing to learn was the legal ins and outs of saving them from being put down for biting someone. It wasn't something I might even have enough time to learn, if one of the pits were the biter. Turning my attention back to the man, I said, "Now answer my... you were at the crime scene last night."

He sat up, brushing dead grass off the front of his pants legs. Definitely the man I'd noticed staring at me so hard. "So were you. Why is the Prince's girlfriend allowed into murder scenes?"

I remembered my private declaration of doing better just in time. Swallowing back the impulse to say "I'm not Thorandryll's girlfriend," I picked a better response. "You have to the count of ten to remove yourself from my property before I call the Sheriff's office."

There was only one kind of person who'd assume I was the elf's girlfriend, and be at a crime scene: a reporter. A dealing-with-the-media plan was yet another thing I didn't have.

He climbed to his feet, keeping an eye on the dogs. "Is your name really Discord Jones?"

I retrieved my cell phone from my windbreaker's pocket. "One."

"I'm Nate Brock, Miss Jones. If you'll just answer a few questions..."

"Two." I knew that name, and dread made my hands tremble. Brock was a reporter who enjoyed digging up dirt on people, and sharing it with the city at large. He'd ruined a few politicians, and apparently took particular delight in tarnishing the reputations of other prominent citizens.

Not a man I wanted interested in me. "Three."

Brock was my height, a slender man under the heavy black, mid-thigh-length coat he wore. "I'm offering you an opportunity here."

Not one I wanted to touch with a ten-foot pole. "Four."

"I'm going." He began to back away, raising his hands. I felt a faint itching sensation in my head, as though something were scratching at the walls of my mental maze. "Not talking to me won't make a difference. You've caught my eye."

"Five." I wanted to throw my phone at him as the itching intensified, and scratch my scalp raw for relief.

"I'll see you around." Brock turned to walk to the driveway. "Maybe you'll feel like talking later."

The intense itching lessened as he moved farther away, and I felt my jaw drop. Nate Brock was a psychic. It was his telepathic attempt to dip into my mind that I'd felt.

No wonder he was so damned good at his job.

"*Why does Leglin get to stay home?*" Bone paused to sniff the bushes.

"Because he's not on the list of dogs people like to demonize." We were on our way over to clan territory. I wasn't risking my Pit Crew or Rufus in light of Brock's unwelcome entry into my life.

"*We were good boys. We didn't bite.*" Diablo nudged my hand. "*We didn't touch him.*"

I stroked his head. "You're the best boys, but some people don't care how good you are."

Not with those scars and missing pieces clearly stating they'd been fighting dogs. Though unscarred, Rufus had the misfortune to be another breed people often considered vicious. "We're not going to take any risks. I love you guys too much."

"*What is 'demonize'?*" Rufus asked as we walked through the arched, stone entrance.

"It's uh, well, it's when someone does something bad, and other people think everyone who looks like that person will also do bad things."

"*Biting?*"

"Biting is one of those things."

The Rottweiler's ears lowered. "*I was trained to bite and hold intruders or attackers, to protect my Master.*"

Which was exactly what he'd done the night before, when the cops had entered Pettigrew's house. I patted his head. "Well, sometimes, biting is okay. But even the times when it's okay, there are people who want to punish dogs that bite. Especially dogs that look like you, or Bone and Diablo."

"*I'm confused.*" Rufus looked it too, the skin on his head wrinkling.

"I'll make it simple. From now on, no biting unless someone's trying to hurt you." I didn't add "or me," because I didn't want a repeat of Red's death. "And I'll do my best to make sure no one ever tries to hurt you. Okay?"

"*Yes, Mistress.*" Rufus trotted ahead to rejoin my Pit Crew, who were sniffing at vehicles as they began negotiating the parking lot.

I'd promised to take care of him the night before, and had just renewed that promise, so it looked like I'd gained another four-legged dependent. But maybe that wasn't a bad thing, even though it'd been a hasty decision. Rufus was a nice dog, and could teach the pits a thing or two about being obedient.

It was a little warmer in the clan's pocket realm. Was learning exactly how pocket realms worked something I needed to do, like yesterday? I decided probably not, but they were something I did need to learn more about before too much longer.

Lost in thought as I attempted to make a list of things I thought I should know now, I was surprised when the dogs veered off the main street to Dane's front yard. My other partner was standing on his front porch, watching Squishy and Speck select potty spots. My Tinies were bundled in their winter coats and intently inspecting potential places.

"Morning," he called.

I turned to walk over. "Morning. Why are you dog sitting?"

"Logan asked me to. He and Terra are, um, discussing her decision to move out. She's moving into the suite in the main building." Dane paused. "With Devon."

"Oh, crap." Logan wasn't fond of Terra's crush.

"Exactly." He gestured at the big dogs. "What's up?"

Squishy noticed Rufus then, and launched herself at him with shrill barks. I couldn't make out half of what she screamed at the Rottweiler while rushing to his defense. Unfortunately, I managed to find Speck's fresh "special spot" right before bending to scoop her up. "Damn it."

Dane laughed. "I'll get some paper towels."

He disappeared inside. I limped toward the porch with Squishy under one arm. "Shush. He lost his master, and you're being really ugly to him."

She grumbled, twisting to give Rufus the Evil Doggy Eye. I sat down on the porch steps, nose wrinkled at the smell of poop, and deposited her into my lap. Dane returned with a wad of paper towels. "Here you go."

"Thanks. Mind holding the Tiny Terror while I clean off my boot?"

"No problem." He took her, and promptly flipped her onto her back in his lap. "I see a little pink tummy."

Pet, pet, pet! She wiggled and whined, her tail wagging.

He caved to her obvious demands while I began wiping dog crap out of the tread of my boot. "I had a visitor this morning. Nate Brock. He's a reporter."

Dane grimaced. "Uh-oh."

"Yeah. The boys flushed him out of the shrubbery."

"I'm guessing he had something to say about that, which is why you brought them here."

"Bingo. Eww, how does one little dog create so much stink?" I carefully folded the first used paper towel. "Is it okay if they stay here during working hours?"

"Sure thing. I'll ask Alanna to let them out, and feed them if we're working late." He tickled Squishy's soft belly, making her squirm in delight.

"Thank you. I hate to impose like this."

"You're clan. It's not imposing." Dane pretended to knock on the side of my head. "When are you going to learn that?"

"I don't know." Because I didn't know exactly what it meant. That was definitely one of the things I should already know. I finished cleaning my boot, and looked across the street and down a bit, at Logan's place. "Should I go stick my nose in?"

He shook his head. "Terra is in full-blown Queen mode right now, and Logan's gone all Protector. None of us butts in when they're like that. Did you call into the office yet?"

Oops. I pulled my cell phone out. "Not yet."

FIVE

"Does he know that you're also a psychic?" Mr. Whitehaven asked after I'd finished filling him in.

"No clue. I've never crossed paths with another human psychic before, at least not that I know of. Just vampires." I watched Rufus lay the piece of bacon Dane had given him in front of Squishy. She pounced on it, furiously wagging her tail.

Dane had cooked breakfast, including two entire packages of bacon. I needed to buy some dogfood for his and Logan's places, or all the dogs were going to become furry chunks. "I can tell you I didn't realize he was psychic until after my brain started itching like crazy. No one's ever reacted when I've telepathically scanned them."

"You said he was among the onlookers at the crime scene last night, and that you used your telepathy then."

"Yes, but that was different. I wasn't trying to get into anyone's heads, just listening in to their louder thoughts flying out. That's a...passive use, not an active one."

Mr. Whitehaven took a few seconds to respond. Enough time for Dane to slip Rufus another piece of bacon without Squishy noticing. "Then all we know for certain is that Mr. Brock's interested in you because of the New Year's Eve ball and spotting you at a crime scene."

"Yep. Thanks, Thorandryll." I made a face, earning a chuckle from Dane. "The thing is, I don't know if there's a difference in how my mental shield feels compared to say, Jo's."

The auburn-haired witch had a natural, thick mental shield, no assembly required. "But I didn't react. Kept my mouth shut."

The boss's smile was present in his voice. "Well done."

"Thank you."

"I'm afraid I don't know what steps we should take on this matter. It's not news that a portion of humans experienced comas of varying lengths during the Melding, or that they woke with magical abilities." Mr. Whitehaven paused. "And we've no idea if last night was the beginning of Mr. Brock's interest in you or not."

Already creeped out by the "telepathic reporter" part, I groaned. "That's not a helpful thought, because it would mean he could've been stalking me for nearly a week and I didn't notice."

"My apologies. I think for now, it's best if you work outside the office until we know more."

"And miss Percy's reaction to a reporter dropping in? Darn." Knowing the parrot, he'd probably poop on Brock's head. "Just kidding. I'm guessing we shouldn't confirm we work for Arcane Solutions if asked."

"Not for now. If you do need to come in for anything, please teleport directly to your office. I'll make certain the door is kept shut."

"Okay. What about last night's case?"

"Continue aiding the police, but be circumspect."

Don't get showy. Check. "Yes, sir."

"It's fortunate your last name is a common one, but it may not be amiss to inform your family about Mr. Brock," the boss said.

Of course. The reporter wouldn't ignore any potential source of information. I cringed, imagining Betty's reaction. "I will."

"The important thing is to remain calm. I must say, you seem to be doing a fine job of that."

"Thanks, but I did consider moving to Tahiti and becoming a beach bum." No point losing my sense of humor over Brock.

Mr. Whitehaven chuckled. "Let's hope such drastic measures won't be necessary. Keep me apprised, Discordia."

"Will do." I ended the call and sighed. "Do I need to repeat anything?"

Dane shook his head. "Stay away from the office unless necessary, answer all questions with 'no comment' or not at all, and act human."

I laughed. "You're a Master of Summing Up."

"Thanks. I'll go see if things are cooled down over at Logan's while you call your parents."

"Okay." My parents weren't the only ones I needed to call.

Logan was quiet as he drove us to the station. Dane wasn't, humming and singing along to the radio while I called Lord Derrick's residence. The vampire was unconscious, it being too early for his six hours of deady-bye to be over. His son, Stone, answered. "Good morning."

"To you, too." The dhampyr sounded cheerful, and I felt bad about the news I had to deliver.

"Oh, excellent. I was about to call you. The guards refused entrance to a reporter a few minutes ago. One that had questions about you."

"Nate Brock?"

"Yes. I've sent guards to the gargoyles' estate, just in case," Stone said, putting a smile on my face.

"Thank you. He's who I was calling to warn you about. Any chance your guards noticed that he's psychic?" I glanced in the review mirror, meeting Dane's eyes. He'd gone silent to listen.

"As a matter of fact, they did mention noticing that. I'm afraid his telepathic attempts to glean information weren't successful." The dhampyr sounded smug.

"Great. Maybe you can answer a question for me. Do you know if constructed mental shields feel different from natural ones?" After all, who else was I going to ask?

"The feel of mental shields varies. Some may feel like walls of brick or metal. Others may feel like thick fog, water, or smoke. If you're asking due to Brock, no, he can't determine another is psychic simply from feeling their mental shield." Stone paused. "He attempted to link to you?"

"Yeah, caught me out on my morning jog. My dogs flushed him out of the bushes."

The dhampyr laughed. "He's determined. I'll grant him that."

"Irritating." One worry laid to rest, or actually three, but now I had another question. "How can he tell if I'm psychic or not?"

"The same way everyone else does. Either knows of you, or has seen you do something that proves it."

"I scanned the crowd at a crime scene last night, and Brock was present."

"Were you just listening, or did you enter minds?"

"Just listened."

"It wouldn't have alerted him, unless you specifically tried to enter his mind," Stone said. "He's not well-practiced in using telepathy around supes, from the sound of it. Both guards were alerted to his attempt by an itching sensation in their minds."

"That's what I felt too. Do non-psychic humans feel that?" No sense wasting the opportunity to learn. Part of the New Me, who was going to do better.

"Not that I've ever heard. Those with natural mental shields are unaware of attempts to breach their minds, unless the attempts are successful. Those without, well, they're the reason we shield ourselves."

A snort escaped me. "Yeah, too noisy. Okay, that's helpful. Thanks."

"If you have the time, I believe my master may be able to offer you some tips."

The offer surprised me. I could use help, and Derrick was extremely powerful in the telepathy department. "Really? That won't break any vampire rules?"

"We're friends," Stone said, a faint lilt making it a question.

"Yes, we are." Another reminder that I needed to get my act together, and start being a friend back to people. But when it came to vampires, where exactly did one begin? Meal planning would be a little difficult. "And I appreciate that."

"As do we. One of us will call and arrange a time to meet."

"Awesome. Thanks again." We ended the call a few seconds later, and I looked at Logan's profile. "Are you mad or sad?"

"Both, and yes, I remember the talk we had about Terra being grown." He gave me a brief, wry grin. "It's different now that she's doing it." He lifted one hand from the steering wheel. "I know, I know. It's her life, her decision to make. I guess I need time to get used to that."

"Or distractions. We have a case, and hey, a reporter running wild." I did jazz hands. "Distractions galore, baby!"

"Oh no, she's getting goofy," Dane said. "We're in trouble now."

"I forgot there's a new guy too. We have Dodson to win over. Maybe I'll puke on his shoes today. That should do the trick." I wasn't looking forward to seeing the new detective again, since I hadn't done much to redeem myself the night before.

"Would you? Please?" Logan's grin was less "oh my God, my baby cousin's grown up" and more "I really, really hope you do that."

"I'll see what I can manage."

"If you toss your cookies, I'm never cooking breakfast for you again." Dane mock-scowled in the rearview mirror at me. "Because that's just rude."

"Well then. Sorry, Logan, I can't be hurting Chef Dane's feelings." Especially since Dane could cook, unlike Logan. I stretched my hands, spreading my fingers wide. "Wonder how many objects Damian's going to have ready for me?"

"We'll know soon enough." Logan signaled to turn into the parking lot. "I have the feeling we'll be ordering lunch in."

SIX

Fortunately, Dodson wasn't there. Neither was Damian, leaving us with Schumacher. "Hello, kiddies. Hope you're ready to work."

We gave him our best smiles, and I said, "That's what we're here for."

"Good, this way. We're set up in one of the interrogation rooms." He led us back out into the hallway, tapping a clipboard against his leg. "Heard an interesting rumor today."

"Did you?" I hoped it wasn't about me.

"Oh, yeah. It seems that a certain elf put in his name for the mayoral election." Schumacher grinned as my mouth fell open. "Yup, that elf, though it's technically not news just yet. Will be by this evening or tomorrow at the latest."

"Are you freaking kidding me?" Thorandryll as mayor of Santo Trueno? It sounded like a terrible idea, and also, like one that could result in more reporters deciding to include me while they scrutinized the elf.

"No joke." Schumacher opened the door of the interrogation room. "Not any more than this is."

The room's table, a 3x6 feet rectangle, was covered in neatly labeled evidence bags. I sighed. "How does he get them to process this stuff so fast?"

"We're definitely ordering lunch in," Logan said.

"Yeah. We also have some new protocols to follow." The detective held up his clipboard. "Notes and we'll be recording."

"Okay." I entered the room and sat down. "Then let's get busy."

The three men joined me, Schumacher sitting across from me with Dane beside him, while Logan sat next to me. Schumacher put his clipboard down. "First, let me tell you how we have to do this. When I start the recording, I'll give my name, blah blah, and after that, state there's a civilian expert present. Wait until I ask, then give your name and specialties."

"General, as in 'I'm a psychic' or what? And what about Dane and Logan?" This was way more formal than usual, and I wondered why the changes had been made.

"I'll mention they're here as support personnel, and they'll each state their names." He leaned forward. "Don't mention where you work, or any psychic abilities not pertinent to what you're doing here. Those are Stannett's exact words."

"Okay. Why?"

"It's part of the agreement your boss and he hammered out." Schumacher leaned back. "And it's a good idea to limit what people can find out."

"Oh." We'd never publicized the fact that Stannett had been used as a curse vessel. Mainly because we hadn't uncovered exactly how Dalsarin had pulled off that particular trick. It looked like Stannett was covering my back in return, making certain I received that reminder. "Okay."

"Ready?"

"Yes." I listened as Shumacher started the recorder and gave the information he'd listed. Then it was my turn: "My name is Discord Jones. I'm a psychic with retro-cognition and psychometry abilities."

The burly detective nodded in approval before mentioning the guys, had them state their names, and explained that they were there as support personnel for me.

"Let's begin with this." Schumacher read off the number on a bag holding an address book, and handed it to me. "Verbal reaction, Miss Jones."

Boy, this was going to take all damn day.

It did. We ordered in lunch and ran past dinner time before clearing the table of evidence. When Schumacher finally turned off the recording device, I leaned back and massaged my temples. "Sorry. Doesn't feel like I was much help."

"You were. Sifting through evidence to find the things that are true evidence takes time." He tapped the box sitting on the table. It held the few things that had really pinged. The rest was in other boxes, stacked against the wall by the door. "The keys were good."

They'd triggered a brief retro-cog vision of Mr. Pettigrew entering his shop, walking to the back room, and noticing the back door was open. There'd been no fear in his surprise, and no sign of any intruder.

"The only problem is, having handled this many objects, if I get something later I won't know which one it's from." I'd mentioned that twice while the recording device was running.

Schumacher nodded. "I know, but the information's the important thing, not whether it came from a box or a pen."

"I'm curious." Dane half-lifted his hand. "Did you pick up any shimmers?"

"Dull, gray dust for Mr. Pettigrew is all."

"What do you mean, 'shimmers'?" Schumacher's brow creased.

"I don't know if it's a separate ability or part of my psychometry, but I usually see a shimmer that represents the owner of whatever stuff I've handled. Dull gray means dead. The shimmer's gold and sparkly if the owner's alive."

He grunted, and began writing. "I'm gonna say it's part of your psychometry. What would happen, if say, my mother gave me a family heirloom. How would you know if the shimmer meant her or me?"

I shrugged, lowering my hands to my lap. "It always represents the current owner. If you gave those keys to an heir, and I handled them again later, I'd get the gold shimmer."

"Why?"

"I honestly don't know. Maybe it's magic. Objects know who they currently belong to, no matter how many times they change hands." I pointed at the box. "Those things still belong to the victim, and they know it."

"But they're inanimate objects," he protested. "How can they 'know' that?"

I thought for a few seconds, and backtracked a little. "Well, maybe it's not so much that the objects 'know' as the owner knows and transfers that fact to them." I leaned over to pick up my purse from the floor and held it up. "This is mine. Every time I grab or am looking for it, that's my thought: my purse. It's going to rub off."

"Now that makes sense, in a weird way. Less woo-woo strange." Schumacher began scribbling away. "If we went to the Evidence Room and you handled stuff for missing person cases..."

"I could most likely tell you whether they were alive or not. As long as I picked up a shimmer." Now there was something really useful I could be doing. "But the downside is, I'd be filling my brain with cases, and they'd interfere with each other until closed. If I had a vision, I wouldn't know which case it belonged to. I mean, unless the vision showed something to make that clear."

Putting his pen down, the burly detective smiled. "Even with limitations, that would be super helpful in closing old cases. Maybe we can work something out when things are slow at the agency."

Since I liked that idea a lot, I smiled back. "Be happy to help. Talk to the bosses and let me know."

"Great. Well," Schumacher looked at his watch and sighed. "It's after eight, and I imagine we'll have another load to go through tomorrow."

"Yay." We all stood up at the same time, and I wasn't the only one stretching. "Where's Damian been all day?"

"Pounding the pavement. Lucky him, Dodson tagged along."

"What's his story?" Logan asked, pulling on his jacket.

Schumacher rolled his eyes. "That asshole was hired at the mayor's request. We're stuck with him, and as you may have noticed, he's not a fan of hocus pocus. 'Hocus pocus' meaning anything and everything to do with supes."

"Short-sighted of him." Logan's hands curled at his sides. "We all have to live together."

The detective gestured with one hand, indicating all four of us. "We know that. Dodson used to be military, honorably discharged about five years ago." His grin was unpleasant. "Heard through the grapevine he was stationed at one of the camps, and thinks the segregation idea is a smart one."

"Awesome. It's going to be a barrel of laughs, working with him." I slung my purse over my shoulder, more interested in food than Dodson's shortcomings.

"I'll pull rank when necessary." Schumacher patted his rather prominent stomach. "Believe it or not, I was once one of the few, the proud. Plus, I have seniority here."

"Good to know." Logan extended his hand, and they shook. "Thank you for your service."

"It was before your time."

"Sure, but without it, who knows how different things would've been?"

Schumacher laughed. "Point taken. You're welcome."

We said our good-byes after promising to be in by ten the next morning. On the way out of the building, I slipped my arm around Logan's. "That was nice of you."

"He's a good guy. People like him are the reason we're not all penned up." Logan planted a quick kiss on the side of my head. "I'm thankful this city didn't panic like some of the others."

"Me too." I had a thought when we reached the car. "But now I wonder how the hell Alleryn set himself up at the hospital. Mom said he was there maybe two weeks after the Melding."

"Glamour." Dane opened the passenger door after Logan unlocked the car. "He glamoured his way in."

"Bet that took some doing." I'd known elves could do more than change their appearance with glamour, such as "persuade" people with it. "Seriously though, there's paperwork and digital records involved. He didn't just appear and glamour everyone into thinking Dr. Allen had been there all along."

Logan waited until we were all in the car before responding. "You'd have to ask him, but my guess is he convinced them to hire him."

"He may have told them the truth." Dane bumped the back of my seat with his knee. "They did need help."

"Uh-huh, an elf telling the truth, straight up?" I laughed. "I'm thinking not."

"Kethyrdryll has been a straight shooter."

I turned enough to look at Dane. "Yeah, except that part where he failed to mention his mom was the Unseelie Queen we were all trying to get to."

Dane made a face. "One instance. He was upfront about everything else."

"True." I turned around. "Of all the elves I've met so far, I trust him the most."

Which actually wasn't saying much, considering my interactions with those other elves, though I did like and trust Kethyrdryll. Alleryn had helped me a lot, but still kept his lips zipped about his original motivation for doing so. He'd made it clear he intended to keep helping me as a friend the one time we'd discussed it.

Kethyrdryll hadn't known I existed until we'd dropped in on him. No secret motivations on his part. Of course, things could've changed since then. Not a happy thought.

"Anyone hungry?" Logan asked, starting the car. "I am."

"I could eat," Dane said. "Pizza?"

Happier topic. "I'm starving. How about Chinese?"

SEVEN

Logan took my side in the Dinner Debate, and Chinese food always made me happy, which helped when the 10 o'clock news opened with the grisly murder of Mr. Pettigrew. They segued directly to announcing, "Prince Thorandryll declared his intention to run for mayor."

"Wow," Dane said. "Horrible murder by possible supernatural assailant, and hey, another supe's going to run for mayor."

"Bet Thorandryll's not happy with that." I reached for the last Crab Rangoon, and my phone dinged. It was a text from Damian. "Oh, crap."

The message gave an address, "Wilkins Warning," and said there were two victims. "Two nights in a row?"

Dane looked at the message. "Isn't that the museum's address?"

It was, and I texted back: **On our way, party of three**. I hoped it wasn't anyone we'd met. Murder scenes were even worse when I knew the victim—no matter how little or well. Logan had already risen and was putting the leftovers away. My phone dinged again, Damian letting me know he'd received my response.

We were on our way less than five minutes later, my dinner already beginning to curdle in my anxious stomach. Logan glanced over at me. "Do they ever call you in on normal murders?"

"Sometimes. Depends on what happened, or if something doesn't strike Damian or Schumacher as quite right, based on the scene."

"Maybe we have another dark elf survivor," Dane said.

"Bite your tongue. One was too many." My shudder wasn't feigned. Dalsarin had been scary, but his personal choice of god, Apep, had been the stuff of nightmares.

"If it is another dark elf, maybe you'll get changed into a different animal this time around." Dane flashed a grin when I looked into the rearview mirror.

"I think it's better I stick to the shape I'm used to. It wasn't much fun, no one knowing who I was." It had been highly aggravating.

"Good point. Did we completely rule out vamps?" Dane aimed his question at Logan.

"I didn't catch any scents but human, blood, and charred meat."

"Wait a minute." I hesitated, my brain working. "You can smell magic, but you didn't when I was a dog. It was magic that changed me."

"It has to be... I guess 'active' is the best word. That magic had done its job."

"Oh." I sighed. "Basically, we can't rule out anyone but humans and shifters."

Dane objected. "Logan said he didn't smell vampire."

"I know, but David made that charm for Nick, when I had the growlies from being a dog. A scent-blocking charm. The killer could be using one too."

"But could that kind of charm conceal the scent of magic?" he asked.

Logan answered. "I don't know. Wouldn't think so, because the charm itself would be magic."

"Okay, let me ask this: Do either of you smell magic when I use my abilities?" I checked their faces, and both shook their heads. "Vampires don't do magic. I mean, not the witch or elf kind. Their abilities are psychic, like mine. I guess that means they do 'natural' magic too, which means, you guys can't smell or sense natural magic."

Logan frowned. "Maybe we'd better ask Damian what he knows about those scent-blocking charms."

"Yeah, we'd better. Hey, at least if a vamp is the killer, we're in good with the vamp council." They'd been working the good publicity for all it was worth. Local public opinion had definitely swayed in their favor. Possibly because Derrick was the perfect poster vamp, with his long, curly hair, boyish face, and lace-cuffed shirts. "If it is a vamp, maybe this case will be solved soon."

No gawkers outside the museum, though I did notice a dark, nondescript sedan parked close to the cop cars and waiting ambulance. A man sat inside it, and looked our way as Logan parked. It was Brock. "The press is here."

"All we can do is ignore him." Logan turned off the engine. "Are you ready for this?"

I could think of an entirely different situation I'd love to hear those words from him, and mentally scolded myself for getting way, way off track. "Not really, but it's not like I have much of a choice."

We left the car, the men careful to put me between them as we walked. I didn't point out that Brock already knew I was here, or that he probably knew Logan's name and other information too. For a few bucks, anyone could run a check on a license plate.

Damian was waiting inside the main doors. "Fair warning, Dodson's here."

"Lovely." I made a vow to keep my dinner down, no matter what. Being laughed at once was enough.

"This way. Didn't your last case involve something stolen from here?"

"Yeah, a magic mirror." Another item for my "Do Better" list. I'd promised the mirror spirit I'd visit, and bring him um, "reading" material. The spirit was a perve.

"Well, a couple of items were stolen tonight as well, from a new exhibit. Dodson's reviewing the security tapes."

Dane and I exchanged a look before I asked, "Which exhibit?"

"Fairy Tales Come to Life."

Of course it'd be that exhibit. "That's the same one the mirror was supposed to be in. What's missing?"

"A stick and pair of boots." Damian stopped at the entrance to an exhibit room. Its door was closed. "Suit up here, please."

We began putting on gloves and shoe coverings. "What do they do?"

"Not a clue yet. The placards are unreadable at the moment." Damian frowned. "Did I tell you this is a Wilkins?"

"Yes, you remembered."

"Maybe we'd better find you a bucket or something."

Ugh. "I'm not going to throw up."

He cocked his head. "Cordi, you nearly always throw up at murder scenes."

"I won't this time." Not in front of Dodson, or where he'd find out. Not when it gave him another chance to insult the crap out of me.

"Okay, it's on your head. If you do, try like hell to get out of the room first."

Involved in reminding my stomach how humiliated we'd felt the night before, I simply nodded. Damian turned and opened the door. Thankfully, the lighting wasn't bright, which made walking in easier.

It was a largish, square room with free-standing display cases scattered around the perimeter. A fancifully designed, white and gold carriage took pride of place in the center. Gore was everywhere, and the smell came close to making my stomach forget our vow. I took little breaths, focusing on the display cases, in particular, the two missing their glass tops. "All these things, and he killed two people for a stick and some old boots?"

"Definitely the same perp." Logan was checking the rest of the room. "Bodies in similar condition."

"What can you smell?" Damian asked.

"Blood, charred meat, and magic. The magic's kind of low-level though, so I think it's probably from the collection."

Dane spoke up. "Do you know how those scent-blocking charms David makes work?"

"They're like ah, well, like an invisible hazmat suit. The wearer is enclosed in a layer of odor neutralizer." Damian paused, his brow wrinkling. "Do you smell citrus of any sort?"

Both shifters sniffed a few times before Logan responded. "Maybe a hint of lemon."

"Then it's possible one was used, but we'll have to check first to see what sort of cleaning chemicals they use here." Damian whipped out his notepad and pen.

"Do you want me to try the display cases?" I really hoped that was the only reason I was here. My stomach and nose were beginning to riot.

"Yes, and they've been processed." My friend was worried, and I could feel it stretching out from him like wispy fingers. He had a reason to be, with similar crime scenes two nights running, and three dead as result.

"Okay." Someone had taped around larger blotches of "stuff," but there were definite footprints around the room. Prints from covered shoes, their tread marks indistinct. I still tried to step around as much of the mess as possible. The scene was relatively fresh, and I winced at the squelch when I had to step on a blood-soaked bit of carpeting. Another wince when I had to step onto the completely shattered bits of glass littering the area around both displays.

The placards were mostly unreadable, thanks to splashes of the victims. One was labeled "The Thieves' Stick", and on the other, only "oots" was legible. Since the museum wouldn't be displaying coots, woots, or toots, Damian's determination of "boots" was likely right. The faint impression of rounded heels and midsoles left on a royal blue display pillow seemed fair confirmation to me. "I'm going to touch the display pillow first."

Damian hustled over, yanking his cell phone out. "Let me video this. Don't take your glove off until I'm ready."

"Okay." Things were definitely changing. "Do I need to state my name and what I'm doing?"

"If you would." He fiddled with his phone, and I looked back at the guys, raising my eyebrows. Dane lifted his hands in a "What can you do?" gesture, while Logan gave a tiny, one-shouldered shrug. "Okay, here we go."

"Discord Jones. I'm going to try psychometry on this display." It took a few seconds to work the glove off my hand. "Ready, one, two, three."

Touching the pillow gave me an instant impression of light weight. I lifted my hand clear. "Sorry. All I picked up was that something not very heavy was on it."

"Let's try the other display."

"Sure." We side-stepped to it, and I checked to make certain he was ready before doing my count. "One, two, three."

The flat surface was cold and free of bits of glass. My psychometry surged, and I saw a dim outline of a stick. "You're right, there was a stick here. I'm not seeing a face or hand though."

Damian turned off the video on his phone with a disappointed look. "Well, thanks for trying."

I felt bad that I wasn't being of much use so far. "Anything else you want to me to try?"

"The only thing else is, um," he gestured around the room. "The victims."

I finally took a good look around the room, and realized the victims weren't hanging from the ceiling. They were on the floor near the rear of the coach, just heads, shoulders, and a few inches of torso. Immediately looking up and closing my eyes, I fought until my stomach subsided. "Okay, get your phone ready again."

"You don't have to do that."

I opened my eyes and met Damian's. "Yeah, I do. Three dead in two days. We don't want this guy running loose any longer than necessary."

He hesitated, searching my face, and finally nodded. "All right. Come with me."

We walked over to the bodies, and Damian checked with the coroner's assistants. They didn't want anyone touching the bodies without gloves. He argued, I worked on keeping my intention firm, and finally, Logan called from his spot by the door, "What if she touches a smaller part?"

"Will that work?" Damian asked, and I nodded.

"It should."

There was more arguing, including calls to Stannett and the coroner, before an agreement was reached. I could try one of the smaller splotches of "stuff"—or "people goop" as someone else called it—but not a partial finger or whatever. And I had to wait until a sample was taken of the splotch they decided on.

The chosen spot of people goop reeked, and I didn't look too closely to see what it was made of. Didn't need to know that, just needed to stick my hand in it and hope we got something worth all the fuss. "Ready?"

Damian was crouched next to me, and he nodded as he steadied his phone. "Go ahead."

"Okay." I had to close my eyes before my hand made contact. The stuff felt cool in temperature. It also felt sticky, and had the texture I imagined fireplaces ashes would, if mixed with enough water. "Nothing yet."

"What's going on?"

I groaned internally. Dodson had joined us.

"I'm sorry, does she have her hand in..." Several people shushed him before he finished, and I silently thanked them. No verbal confirmation about having my hand in liquefied people needed, especially when I realized the goop felt warmer than it first had.

"I think..."

"Holy shit," someone said, and I opened my eyes as Damian grabbed my wrist.

"What?" It felt like something was beginning to trickle down from my hair.

"Get something to wipe her hand off now!" He yanked my hand upward.

A swooping sensation was followed by a rush of heat flaring upward from my feet, and I blinked as the trickling sensation reached my eyes. "I don't know..."

I didn't finish, because of intense, burning pain. A haze of red descended as I began to flail, trying to get away from Damian's grip. Someone grabbed me around the waist from behind as I half-stood, and there was screaming, yelling, and everything was red and gold and black.

Blinded, I was aware of being carried, and then coldness enveloped my gloveless hand. My mouth was open, my throat felt raw. I was the one screaming, could taste smoke and blood. For once, I didn't pass out, and I really, truly regretted that since I was being roasted alive.

Two hands touched my face, and the vision ended, leaving me sucking in air and blinking. There was blood in my eyelashes, and whoever had grabbed me still had hold, my feet not touching the ground. Logan and Dane were in front of me. Both were touching my cheeks, and anxiously checking my eyes.

My hair looked wet, and my clothing felt soggy. I was up just high enough to be looking slightly down at the guys. Damian was frantically dabbing at my hand, and I noticed that my skin was pink and blistered. It didn't hurt, but my voice was hoarse. "I'm okay."

The chest my back was against rumbled, and Dodson said, "Jesus Christ, woman."

"Sorry. You can put me down now."

He did, slowly, and took a step back. Dane lowered his hand to my arm, offering support if I needed it. Logan kept his hand on my cheek, and I managed to give him a small, quick smile. Quick, because it occurred to me that I was actually covered in blood. "Oh. That's blood. My blood?"

"Don't know."

"You're all burned," Damian said. "You're actually burned."

"It doesn't hurt." I felt a little woozy, but otherwise, remarkably okay for nearly being burned alive. Or a close, psychic approximation of it. "I can't ride in your car like this."

Disbelief flashed across Logan's face before he laughed. "Don't worry about my car. Are you okay?"

"I think so." Gently pulling my hand out of Damian's grasp, I flexed it and took a closer look. Yep, there were small, clear blisters all over my newly pinkened skin. I pulled my coat sleeve up, and the blisters continued up my arm. "Is my face blistered too?"

"Yes. I am so sorry, Cordi." Damian was quivering with guilt, the corners of his lips downturned.

"I'm okay, really. Nothing hurts. Well, my throat, but other than that..."

"What in the hell just happened?"

I turned around to look at Dodson, Logan and Dane moving to be ready in case I passed out or something. At least, I thought that's what they were doing. The big detective looked a little pale, and the front of his clothing was smeared with blood. His eyes looked slightly wild too.

Though such visions weren't all that regular, and I'd definitely never had one of being burned alive before, I couldn't resist assuming a nonchalant tone. "Sometimes, psychic stuff goes all out. That's what happened. I got a minute of reliving what those poor men went through."

Dodson stared at me, and I wished I could see myself. It had to be sight that wouldn't soon be forgotten. I probably looked like Carrie after the pig blood had been spilled on her. Behind him, the others were gathered around the door, also staring at me.

I shrugged. "Sorry. I don't know in advance what's going to happen. Even sorrier, because it didn't give us anything useful."

Dodson opened his mouth, closed it and looked down at his shirt. He looked at me, grunted, and turned around. "Show's over. Back to work."

EIGHT

Strangely entranced, I stared in the mirror. Where in the hell had all the blood come from? Even my pea coat was soaked in it. The only item of clothing it hadn't soaked through were my boots, but from the feel of it, my socks hadn't escaped the deluge.

"You okay in there?" Logan asked from the doorway of the restroom. He was keeping the door from closing, to keep an ear on things. I didn't think I was in danger of passing out, as the woozy feeling had passed.

"Yeah." I finally turned the water on, happy the museum hadn't upgraded to the water-saving, auto sensor type faucets. After peeling off my remaining glove, the interior of which was bloody, I began washing both hands. The pinkness was fading from my skin. I hoped the blistering disappeared as fast.

"Kind of thinking touching the dead is not a great idea for you."

"Can't really argue with that." But I'd probably do it again, somewhere down the line. "What did it look like to you?"

"An explanation of why there's been fresh and cooked blood. It was seeping down, out from your hair at first. After Dodson picked you up, it looked like it was coming from every pore. The blisters appeared just a second after that."

"What can cause that?"

"I don't even have an idea," he said. "I see Dane coming back."

He'd gone out to the car to grab Logan's bag from the trunk. Shifters, at least those of my clan, tended to keep extra clothing on hand for emergencies. I was in luck, because this time, Logan's extras were sweats. They'd be too big, but at least they'd be dry.

"I'm going to need a trash bag for my clothes." I hoped the blood would wash out of everything, and congratulated myself on not succumbing to the "Women in Leather" stereotype. I could only imagine how difficult peeling off blood-soaked leather pants would be.

"We'll find one."

"Hey, and maybe one of those dust cloths to dry off with?" I'd need more than paper towels for my hair in particular, assuming I could figure out how to rinse it in the shallow sink.

"Sure." Logan followed that with, "Thanks."

"No problem," Dane said. "Does she need anything else?"

Logan gave him my requests, and our partner went off in search of both items. I went to the door to take the bag, holding out my other hand for his inspection. "I think it's fading."

He looked at my hand and my face before nodding. "It is, but maybe we should call Alleryn and have him look you over."

I hesitated, but then I could quiz the healer about his Prince's sudden political aspirations. Of course, I had an idea about them, but confirmation would be nice. Plus, getting a checkup would put a stop to the worried vibes zinging off Logan, Dane, and Damian. Those vibes were getting annoying, like little electrical shocks. "Okay. I guess ask him if he'll meet us at my place."

"Will do."

Dane returned with a big, black trash bag and a clean, folded dust cloth. "Here you go, Bloody Mary."

"Hah. You're funny. Thanks." I was careful to keep both clear of my clothing. "Okay, time to shut the door and make certain no one busts in on me."

"They'll have to go through us first," Dane promised with a grin. "I bet Dodson thinks you're a badass now, after how quickly you went from screaming to cool as a cucumber."

I had to smirk a little, feeling smug I'd recovered so quickly. "Be out in a bit."

Door shut, I went back to the sink area, put the bags and dust cloth down, and began undressing. Each item went into the trash bag immediately, though I stuffed my bra and panties underneath my jeans and shirt.

Naked, I backed up to take another look in the mirror at the blood smeared all over me. For just a minute, fear took hold. What if the vision hadn't been a psychometry effect, but a precognition?

I shook my head at my mirror self. *Don't go borrowing trouble, Cordi.*

Nearly an hour later, I stepped out of the restroom with the duffle and half-full trash bag. Dane immediately offered to take both, and I let him. Not knowing if it was my blood or not, I'd put both used paper towels and the dust cloth in the trash bag. My boots were in the bag too, leaving me to walk around in my borrowed socks. I'd skipped donning Logan's boxers, surprised to find a pair included since the one time I'd helped him undress, he hadn't been wearing any. Well, none had been in his jeans when I pulled them off him.

"Now what?"

"Damian wants us to look at the security tape," Logan replied.

I made a "don't really want to" face. "Experiencing a little of it was kind of enough for me."

"Then we'll tell him that, and take you home."

We set off for the security office, and found both detectives and a uniformed officer there. The maroon smears decorating Dodson's clothing apparently bothered him, because he was brushing at one on his shirt when we walked in.

"Hey."

Damian spun around, scanning my face. His brightened. "You don't look as burned."

"It's fading, but Logan called Alleryn and I'm going to get checked over. Pretty sure I'm fine though," I added when another dart of worry zoomed from him. I hated asking in front of Dodson, but did anyway. "You don't want me to watch their deaths, do you?"

"Of course not. But I do want you to watch just before, and what happened after. If you feel up to it?"

That I could do. "Sure."

"Okay, have a seat." He nodded at the uniformed cop, who began tapping away. A second later, I was seated and watching the screen. A lump rose in my throat when I recognized one of the security guards as they walked into the room with alert expressions. It was Ernie, the sixty-something man who'd shown us the video of the magic mirror's theft.

They split up after entering, each covering a side of the room, and halted at the back of the coach to converse. There were head shaking and shrugs. Whatever they'd heard or seen, no one else was in the room with them.

All of a sudden, both men went rigid, their stiff bodies floating upward until they were three or four feet off the ground. "Pause that."

The cop did, and I studied the image closely. Nothing indicated an invisible being had grabbed and lifted them. "Telekinesis."

"Jump ahead," Damian ordered. It took a second for the cop to find the right point, and we watched as the glass tops of the display cases exploded. Once the glass settled, a pair of dark brown, leather boots went floating out of sight, followed by the stick from the other case.

"Telekinesis again, and the cause of death has to be pyro-kinesis. I don't know how the killer does the blood thing." I sat back, sickened by the idea of someone using psychic abilities to murder innocent humans. "With telekinesis, there's no need for him to kill anybody. Why is he?"

"He wants blood." Dodson brushed at his shirt again, his eyes on the screen. "We're probably looking at a vampire."

"The vamp council has rules about killing humans." Look at me, defending the very beings I'd once been happy to turn to ash for any reason. My, how things had changed. "If the killer's a vamp, he or she has gone rogue."

"Could this be political then?" Damian's brow was furrowed when I turned the chair to look. "Maybe a vamp trying to prove he or she is beyond the council's control?"

"I couldn't tell you, but I can talk to Lord Derrick. Tell him it's possible there's a rogue, and I bet the vamp council will turn the Barrows upside down, looking for one. Of course, if they don't find him or her, it'll either be because the killer's not a vampire, or the killer's not staying in the Barrows to avoid being found out."

"Right." My friend nodded.

Dodson was brushing at his shirt, his blue eyes moving from the screen to Damian. "She can't just go blab about the case to vampires."

"I don't know how they did it where you're from, but here, we're committed to working with the various supernatural law personnel." Damian dismissed him with a cool glance. "I'll talk to Stannett, and let you know if he okays it, Cordi."

"Sure. Anything else you need from us tonight?" Exhaustion was beginning to set in, along with a super-sized headache.

"No, go on and get checked over. Let me know what the healer says."

"Sure thing." I got up, and Damian touched my arm.

"Thank you for trying, and I'm sorry the experience was painful."

I moved enough to peck him on the cheek and smiled. "It's okay, all part of the psychic package. I'll text you later."

"All right. Bye."

We left, Dane slinging the trash bag with my soggy clothing over one shoulder. "Well, this has been an interesting night. You planning to grill Alleryn about Thorandryll?"

I had to cover a yawn, wincing because it caused a spasm of pain. "I was, but man, I'm tired."

"I'd ask, but he ignores me. He'll speak to Logan."

Pushing the main door open, and nodding to the officer on watch duty, Logan uttered a soft snort. "He keeps our conversations limited to orders and snarky remarks."

The concrete's cold seeped through my borrowed socks after my first two steps outside. I swallowed my first reaction to Logan's statement, which was "Well, he is an elf," and frowned. "Not nice of him."

"Elves don't see a reason to be polite to those below them, which is all non-elves. Minus a few exceptions." Logan stiffened. "He's leaning on my car."

"Alleryn?" I peered at the parking lot. "Oh, Brock."

The reporter was leaning against the back of Logan's car, and didn't move when we approached. He was too busy studying me, and I wasn't comfortable with his scrutiny. I hadn't felt silly until then, in my borrowed clothing and shoelessness.

"Miss Jones, Mr. Sayer. Care to comment on what's going on tonight?"

Logan's response was short and succinct. "Get off my car."

"No comment," I added to his demand.

Brock smiled, and moved, his attention turning to Dane. "Don't believe we've met yet. I'm Nate Brock."

Dane just looked at him while Logan checked the dark, glossy green paint for scratches. Not finding any, he shot Brock a flat, unfriendly look before unlocking the trunk for Dane to toss the bags in.

"Weren't you wearing something different when you arrived, Miss Jones?" The reporter's eyes were back on me, and I hoped I hadn't missed any spots of blood. "What happened to your face?"

"No comment." I'd forgotten the blistering.

Brock grinned. "Any comment on your boyfriend deciding to run for mayor?"

Dredging up my sweetest smile, I repeated, "No comment."

"Benjamin Jones, that's your father, right? And ah, Sunshine Jones, she's your mother?"

Damn, he worked fast. It took every ounce of self-control I had to keep smiling. "No comment."

He shook his head. "Lack of cooperation seldom works in my subjects' favor, Miss Jones."

My brain began to itch. Brock was trying to get into my mind. Logan slammed the trunk lid hard enough to shake the car, and I jumped.

The reporter just looked at him. "Nice car, Mr. Sayer. Did you restore it yourself? You're a mechanic, right? Have a garage in the Palisades?"

Dane herded me to the passenger door. Logan pretended Brock didn't exist, walking around the reporter to the driver's door.

"How about you, young man? Are you a mechanic too? Why would the police need a couple of mechanics at a crime scene?" Brock paused before firing off one more question as we were getting into the car. "And why does the Prince's girlfriend need two mechanics escorting her around?"

I'd gotten into the backseat, because Dane wouldn't, and sighed as both men shut the car doors. "He's good."

"He's irritating." Logan started the car. "And he'd better move."

Brock did, and the mental itching began to fade. I turned to watch him, trying to estimate the distance between us. "Don't back out yet."

"Why?"

"I'm checking something. Did either of you get an itchy brain?"

They replied in stereo, "No."

"Good." The itchy sensation stopped completely, and I turned around. "About forty feet. That's his telepathic range."

"Helpful to know." Dane twisted in the front seat, hooking his arm around the headrest. "Do you catch brain chatter from us all the time?"

I had to think about it, and finally shook my head. "Actually, I don't think I do. I catch emotions sometimes, but I think most of the telepathic contact has been direct. I listen for you guys to think at me."

"Logan's driving, so try doing to me what Brock was trying to do to you."

"Dude, I don't pick brains like that. Especially not my friends' brains. It's rude."

Dane laughed. "I know you don't, but I'm asking for a good cause. I want to know if I have a secure brain or not, and if I do, how secure it is."

I hesitated, feeling it was wrong to even think about breaking into a friend's mind. That was way different than simply listening to thoughts flying out of people's heads, or "dipping" into the minds of those without any mental shielding to speak of, in order to glean information. "I don't know."

"You won't be doing anything wrong, because I'm asking you to do it." He smiled. "I think it's important we find out if it's possible for Brock to get inside my head."

He had a point, and I reluctantly agreed. "Okay, but let's be clear: I am not comfortable doing this."

"Noted, and sorry I'm asking, but I really think it's necessary."

"You do realize that if someone with psychometry touched you, they could find stuff out that way, right?" Though, come to think of that, I couldn't recall my psychometry reacting much when I touched shifters. Only a single, vivid episode with Patrick, Nick's older brother came immediately to mind. "It's a gate opener for other abilities."

"Sure, but I'm thinking telepathy is the big issue. Most vamps have it." Dane flicked his fingers. "You have it, Brock has it. Could be wrong, but I'm thinking that means telepathy's a pretty common ability."

Another good point. He was just full of them tonight. "I guess so. Okay, ready?"

"Yes."

NINE

I'd established a telepathic link with Dane before, to transfer a memory from him to Leglin. That had been with my partner's cooperation, and his intent focus on the appropriate memory.

This time, Dane wasn't being cooperative, and my linking attempt ran smack into a wall. "You do have a natural shield."

"See if you can break through it."

"I don't think that's a good idea, because I don't know what could happen. I might break your shield permanently, or give you an aneurysm, or who knows what?"

"Logan's here," Dane said. "He can help me shift, and I'd heal."

I appealed to Logan. "I don't think it's safe. I'm used to scanning and talking. This is way different."

He glanced in the rearview mirror at me. "We trust you."

Maybe they shouldn't about this particular thing. Technically, no one was safe from a powerful, skilled telepath, including less powerful telepaths. Hence my running as fast as possible away from Derrick the first time we crossed paths. If I threw modesty to the winds, then I counted as a powerful telepath, but as a skilled one? Not so much.

Dane was watching me. "Come on, Cordi."

"Okay, fine." I huffed out a breath. "But if it starts to hurt, say something so I can stop."

"Promise."

Everyday imagery worked far better than trying to visualize tiny electrical pulses flowing around in brain coral. It was freaky enough, being able to "see" and "hear" other people's minds, so the simpler the imagery, the easier it was to make sense of having telepathy.

I'd learned that "personal bubbles" were a real thing for minds, not just bodies. Everyone, myself included, was the center of their own little, round universe. Which meant that mental shields tended to be circular in nature. Dane's wasn't an exception to that rule. Huh, maybe that's why Sal suggested a maze to me?

Afraid of causing real damage, I carefully circled his mental wall twice, before noticing a line in one spot. Closer examination revealed it wasn't the only line, and together, they formed the outline of a door. I gave it an experimental push, and nothing happened.

"Did you feel that?"

"What?" Dane replied. "Are you doing something?"

"Yeah. Tell me if you notice or feel anything." I gave the door a harder push. No reaction from him.

Maybe the door didn't push open. There wasn't a handle for pulling, just a smooth surface, aside from the shallow indentions of the door's outline.

Hm. I imagined my telepathic links as power cords, because I was basically plugging into their minds. Made sense to me, but confronted with Dane's "door," I began to rethink that imagery decision. Maybe a rope was a better? Because a rope could unwind to become more than a single piece.

Yeah. My link changed from a power cord to a thick rope, the end of which unraveled into four separate strands. They slid around each line of the door, and found tiny holds. *Hah!*

I pulled, and nothing happened except Dane blinked. "Did you feel that?"

"No, had one of those see-something-from-the-corner-of-my-eye moments."

Huh. Another pull, and he blinked again. "Did the same thing just happen?"

"Yeah," Dane said.

I smiled. "I think you have an early warning system. Anytime 'corner-of-the-eye' visitors happen in batches, good chance someone's trying to break through your mental shield."

"Now that's cool, and important to know."

"Yeah." I gave the link a hard yank, saw him blink, and felt the door open just a touch. Enough for the four-pieced link to slither through, and Boom! I was in his brain. "How about now?"

"A third C.O.E. visit, but nothing else." My grin tipped him off. "Oh, you're in my head right now?"

"You keep pushing your pizza every day agenda just to annoy me. Pest."

Dane laughed. "Okay, you're in my head."

"Yeah. It wasn't exactly easy." I reeled the link in, and his mental door shut. My head was really beginning to pound. "And I'm out."

"Guess I'd better work on that." Dane turned and settled into his seat. "Think Brock can break in?"

"I don't know. Stone doesn't think he's had that much practice with supes." We'd made it to the highway, and would be home in minutes. "Hope Alleryn's there, and hasn't had to wait too long. I could sure use one of his pain remedies."

The elf was there, waiting behind the wheel of a silver SUV that probably cost almost as much as my house. Alleryn hopped out the second Logan finished parking, opening the passenger door to look in. "What happened? Those are burn blisters. You still have hair, so I'd assume you weren't the centerpiece of a bonfire."

"Mind if we get out?" Dane asked, leaning away from him. Without a word, Alleryn moved back. "Thank you."

Once out of the car, I recounted the pertinent events on the way to the house, finishing as we reached the dining room table. The elf listened, his grass green eyes intent on the visible blisters.

"It's rare, a psychic experiencing physical manifestations of trauma, but not completely unheard of. Is this the first time it's occurred?"

"No." I told him about my first, and possibly only, precognition while Dane dumped my clothing in the washer, started coffee, and began poking around in the fridge. Logan sat at the table with us, watching Alleryn. Something he'd probably done every time the elf had worked on me.

"They looked much worse at first, yes?" Alleryn examined the back of my hand, lightly running a fingertip over the remaining blisters.

"Yeah. My skin was shiny pink and I think they were bigger."

"They should disappear in a few hours on their own. Are you feeling any discomfort?"

"Big headache, nothing else."

He nodded, made a little gesture, and Logan's sniff sounded right before an old-fashioned, black medical bag appeared on the table. "I'll mix a draught for you."

"I'd appreciate it, and thank you for coming over so late."

Alleryn waved away my thanks, and stood to open his bag. "Have you heard the news?"

"'Mayor Thorandryll'? Yeah, it just doesn't have that certain ring to it." I accepted a cup of coffee from Dane. "Mm, thanks."

He gave Logan the other cup he carried, and asked the elf, "Would you like a cup of coffee?"

Alleryn nodded, pulling out little glass bottles. I cleared my throat. "You know, it's considered polite to reply verbally."

He paused to look at me. One of his eyebrows rose. "Beg pardon?"

"We're friends. These two aren't only my friends, but part of my clan. I like it when all my friends can play nicely with each other."

The elf blinked, glanced at Logan then Dane. Both smiled at him. "You're saying my manners are lacking."

"Yes, that's what I'm saying."

"My apologies." Alleryn inclined his head to me before looking at Dane. "Yes, I would enjoy a cup, and thank you for offering."

"You're welcome, and I'll have it ready in just a minute." Dane didn't look or sound smug, but he did wink at me while turning away.

Alleryn returned to selecting bottles. "Not that I mind making house calls, but this is a relatively simple remedy. It does work best freshly mixed, but the ingredients are easily obtainable."

"Great, if you'd write..." was as far as I got.

"Considering the condition you're often in when needing one of these, I don't think you're the best choice as student." The elf looked across the table at Logan. "You're a much better choice."

Aw, he was trying. I sat back and sipped my coffee, watching Logan move to the elf's side. Herbs were named, Alleryn pausing to politely thank Dane again when his coffee was delivered. Measurements were in pinches, dashes, and drops.

I followed along until Dane asked, "Do you want me to go get the dogs?"

"I can have Leglin bring them home, but they'd probably enjoy the walk if you don't mind."

"I don't." With a pat to my shoulder, he left. The touch reminded me that my latest vision had ended when they'd both touched me. Coincidence?

I didn't know, and having an elf handy, decided to ask. Not until they'd finished and Logan left the table to check my fridge for something to mix the result into.

"Maybe you can answer a question for me."

Alleryn flipped his mahogany hair over his shoulders. "I'll try."

"It's about visions. Do they stop only when they decide to?"

"I'm far from an expert on the subject, but there is an old story that's relevant. It's said there once was a mage who was plagued by visions. They near filled his waking hours, and the poor man couldn't touch a thing without having a vision result." He paused, noticing Logan holding up a carton for approval. "Yes, juice is fine. Just a small glass."

"What happened to him?"

Alleryn began putting his little bottles away, checking the cork stoppers on each before placing them in the bag. "After years of suffering, someone gave him a cat. The cat proved able to sense when his master was in distress, and would run to him when the visions held sway. Whether it was the physical contact or purring, I can't say, but the mage's visions rapidly began to lessen in both intensity and quantity."

Interesting. I decided to tell him about something else. "I've recently pulled a few people into my visions. Not just people, but Leglin too."

Alleryn sat down, his face going slack. He rallied and leaned forward. "That's not usual. However, blood magic is quite powerful, and the hound is blood-bonded to you. Which people?"

"Logan, Dane, and Moira."

"Members of the clan by which you are tied by blood." He nodded, straightening to push the small bowl holding the results of their efforts to Logan. "Just mix it in well, and it's ready. It must be the blood bonds, but that's not actually pertinent to your question."

I'd finished my coffee, and put the cup down. "The vision tonight stopped when he and Dane touched me. One second, I was burning, the next, I was fine. Well, aside from looking burned and having a sore throat from screaming."

"Fascinating." Alleryn abruptly turned to Logan. "What were you thinking?"

Logan froze, spoon an inch above the powdery surface of the juice. "What?"

"When you touched her. What were you thinking?"

My boyfriend—too soon? Had I been calling him that?—began to stir. "She was screaming with pain, and I wanted her to stop hurting."

"You touched her, and she did. Hm." The elf leaned back, tapping his chin with one long finger. "Could be coincidence. Or not. Perhaps the blood ties? Then again, it may be something far simpler."

"As in?" It was kind of fun, watching Alleryn think. The chin tapping, his eyes darting around, and even his eyebrows got in on the act, twitching up and down. He wasn't a quiet thinker. More like a toned down, mad scientist thinker.

"Love." He practically trilled the word. I met Logan's eyes, and we both found something else to do. He stirred, and I admired the shiny surface of my dining table.

Alleryn laughed. "Really? You're both adults. But I didn't necessarily mean the romantic sort. There are others: the love of a parent for a child, vice versa, and etcetera. Friends care for one another, and that's yet another sort."

"Dane would've been thinking the same thing," Logan said. "Friends and clan. Cordi is one of our queens."

The elf pointed at him. "Exactly, and you male tigers do have that instinctive urge to protect your queens."

It sounded logical, but of course, we didn't know whether or not it had been a coincidence. "I guess we'll have to test that theory next chance we have."

"Please do, and let me know the results." Alleryn beamed. "If it works, it could be helpful to the others."

"Uh, what others?" I watched his smile dim.

"There are only a few, and the cat idea didn't work for them. Neither did dogs, rabbits, or horses. We even tried llamas and alpacas."

It sounded as though I'd been right to fear being stuck permanently in a vision. "Are you saying that there are psychics having constant visions right now?"

"Five, over the entire world. At least, only five that my colleagues and I know of. We've been trying to help them without success. But if this," he waggled his hand between Logan and me, "works, I'll suggest we attempt a blood bond to a service dog."

I wished there were something handy guaranteed to trigger a strong vision. Oh, but wait. We'd be at the station tomorrow, and they had murder weapons galore. "I'll see about arranging opportunities for another strong vision."

Logan brought me the juice, which had a herb-flecked froth on top. "Here you are, madame."

"Thank you." I downed it. "Delicious. Orange juice is definitely preferred from now on."

"Noted." He took the glass back with a grin, and went to the kitchen.

"Perhaps not too strong of a vision," Alleryn said. "I don't know how the physical manifestations may affect you over time."

"Do the ones having constant visions ever have them?"

"It's rare," he reminded me. "You're the first to have them that I know of, since the Sundering."

Discord Jones, head of the psychic class. I was just too lucky.

TEN

Dane arrived with all the dogs shortly after Alleryn finished his coffee and left.

Six dogs. I was in danger of becoming an animal hoarder. The thought struck my funny bone, making me giggle. My mind was getting fuzzy from the pain remedy.

"Go on home," Logan told Dane. "And thanks. I'll get everyone tucked in and lock up."

"Okay." Dane ruffled my hair in passing. "Night, Cordi."

"Night night." I waved at him, knowing my smile was goofy, but not really caring. Elf meds were better than prescription drugs and all-natural, to boot.

He chuckled, waving back. "You're drunk. Go to bed."

"Drugged." There *was* a difference.

"Yeah. See you tomorrow." He left, quietly shutting the front door behind him.

"I'll help you upstairs before cleaning up down here." Logan held out his hand.

"You don't have to clean. I can do it tomorrow." I completely missed trying to take his hand, and laughed. "No Coordination Cordi is in the house."

Bone reared to plant his front paws on my thigh. "*You smell funny. Like blood and plants.*"

"It's been one hell of a night."

"*And Chinese food.*" His one ear went flat, and every pair of dog eyeballs present began burning a hole in me. "*Did you save us any?*"

I looked up at Logan. "They want Chinese food."

"It's after three. They can wait. Come on, sweetheart. You're going to be out cold in a few minutes."

"Okay."

"*Not fair,*" Bone muttered, but he dropped to all fours. The others, except for Rufus and Leglin, complained too.

"Sorry, guys."

Logan pulled me to my feet, and I swayed. "Maybe I'd better carry you."

"That is a fantastic idea." I had a better one. "I have one too. You could stay here tonight."

He swooped me up and the room spun. "You're wearing my emergency pajamas."

"Oh." I had to think about that for a second. "I can change."

Logan chuckled, heading for the stairs. "If you can manage to change, I'll stay."

"Yay." I let my head fall to his shoulder. "Cuddling."

Upstairs, he deposited me on the bed and followed my increasingly slurred directions to retrieve panties and a PJ set. "Here you go. I'll settle the dogs and lock up."

"Uh huh." I began struggling with the drawstring on the sweatpants.

"Let me get that." Logan made short work of the slipknot. "Okay, you're good to go."

"Thank you," I sang, and he left the room laughing.

My mission was simple: change clothes. Completing it wasn't so simple. I couldn't get my fingers to work well, as more fuzz filled my mind. A sudden ear bug had me trying to remember the words to "Mary Had a Little Lamb." I sang the words I knew and made nonsense noises to fill the gaps.

The sweats were relatively easy, though I somehow managed to stick my head in a sleeve while pulling off the top. My sleeveless PJ shirt went on without trouble, but I had my panties to my knees before realizing both legs were in a single leg hole. Reversing, I fixed that issue while laughing at myself.

Once they were properly on, I blew hair off my forehead while regarding the shorts. Putting those on seemed like overkill, and way too much trouble. I shoved them under my pillow and managed to navigate my way under the covers.

I was out like a light maybe three seconds later.

Half-awake, I snuggled closer to Logan, happy to have a cuddle buddy. "You stayed."

"We had a deal." He sounded drowsy, and patted my arm, which was across his waist. His other arm was trapped between us. "My arm's asleep."

"Sorry." I kissed his shoulder and rolled onto my back. "I slept like a log."

"Not exactly."

I froze in mid-stretch. "Oh?"

He opened his eyes and turned his head, the seriously cute grin I loved appearing on his face. "Don't worry, nothing you said while under the influence will be held or used against you."

Oh, hell. What had I said? "I don't remember anything."

"That's probably for the best." The flecks of gold in his eyes seemed to be dancing. "But the part about rap music was funny."

I didn't like rap music, so why would I even talk about it? "What did I say about it?"

Logan sat, rearranged his pillow against the headboard, and scooted until his back was against it. "I'm very clear on the fact that you don't have any appreciation for that particular musical form."

I winced. "And?"

"You made up your own rap, consisting of all the things you find offensive about it." He tilted his head. "Words were said that I didn't know you used."

I groaned, and pushed myself into sitting position. Unable to see his face, I scooted around to sit tailor-style. "Sorry. I hope I didn't let fly with too many F-bombs."

"All I'm gonna say is, don't plan on a rap career. Most of your songs would be bleeped out when played on the radio."

I cringed. "What else did I say?"

Logan's grin left the premises. "You told me how awful you've been feeling about not meeting all of your responsibilities, and swore that you were trying to do better."

"Oh." I hadn't meant to publicize it. That frigging pain remedy apparently did double duty as a truth serum. "Well, yeah. I've been slacking on some things."

"I think you're doing fine, under the circumstances." Logan made a face. "We had a little argument about it."

Our first argument, and I didn't remember a word of it. "I'm sorry."

"It's okay. You're allowed to feel how you want to about things. But I do think you're too hard on yourself, and I'm allowed to have that opinion. I'm just going to be more careful about sharing it, because you gave me an earful." He patted my knee.

Ouch. I could only imagine myself ranting without filters, and it definitely sounded like none of mine had been working last night. "I'm really sorry."

Logan reached for my hand, and I gave it to him with a flutter of relief. Still wanting to hold hands was a good sign I hadn't blown it between us. "Honesty's nothing to apologize for."

"Being ugly is."

He chuckled. "You weren't ugly, just adamant."

"Well, that's a relief. How else did I embarrass myself?"

His grin flickered back to life. "Well, the subject of sex did come up."

I covered my eyes with my free hand and groaned again. "Oh God. I didn't."

"Does that mean you don't want particulars?"

Did I? Not really, but then again, I kind of needed to know what the hell I'd said to him. "What did I say?"

"You informed me that you're on birth control, and haven't had sex without using condoms, too."

That wasn't so bad, and happened to be completely true. Bonus: Now I didn't have to have that conversation while sober and tripping all over myself in embarrassment. I dropped my hand from my eyes. "Okay, true."

Logan's expression was serious. Maybe I'd uncovered my eyes too soon. "You also pointed out that since I'm sterile and a shifter, condoms weren't necessary now."

Oh, holy crap on toast. "That was a terrible thing to say. I'm..."

"I told you that I was sterile. It's a fact. Don't apologize for repeating a fact." He lightly squeezed my hand. "And now I also know that you're not keen on the idea of having children."

Boy, drugged Cordi was a giant blabbermouth. I needed to stick to my mom's headache tea from now on. "Oh."

"It's fine. Not an issue."

"But you..."

"Yeah, we talked about that too. Finding out the cause of my sterility doesn't mean it can be reversed. I don't expect to father children, Cordi."

"But if you could, you'd want them."

He shook his head. "It's not my choice. I don't have to go through growing a new person, labor, and delivery."

Good night, he was making my little heart go pitter-pattering all over the place. "It wouldn't be fair though."

"Relationships are about compromising, and sometimes, sacrificing. I don't think anything's going to change on that front, so it's not either of those. If it did happen to change, well, I've never expected kids anyway."

Logan sounded really certain, but I had to be sure, and so far, was amazed at how well I was handling such a serious conversation. I was maintaining eye contact and everything. "You may feel differently, if it did change."

"Maybe," he said. "But I'm not going to throw away whatever we have going at that point. You may feel differently then, too. If you don't, that's fine. I know where you stand on the subject, and it's not a deal-breaker for me."

The wall I'd felt between us was gone, just like that. I realized that I'd probably put it there. "Is it okay if I feel really relieved right now?"

Logan smiled. "Absolutely."

"Good, because I think I love you, and I was scared the kid thing would mean no more us." I paused, lips parted, and replayed what I'd just said. "Oh, that was..."

"Honest." He lifted my hand and kissed it. "I think I love you too."

My lips curved into a huge smile. Maybe, just maybe, being an adult wasn't so hard all the time.

ELEVEN

"Sorry we're late," I said to Damian, who hugged me.

"You forgot to text me last night. You look fine though."

My blistering was completely gone. "I am, and sorry for forgetting. Alleryn gave me something for my headache, and I kind of went loopy before passing out."

"I apologize too. I should've let you know she was okay," Logan said.

"All good now." Damian grinned. "Actually, you look really good, Cordi. Rested and unstressed. That's a first in a long time."

Truthfully, I felt rather amazing. Ready to take on the world, or at least, every bad guy in town. "I'm in a great head space today."

"Fantastic." Damian squeezed my shoulders before dropping his hands.

Noticing Dodson leaning against a file cabinet, watching us, I walked over. "Thank you for helping me last night. I'd like to pay for the dry cleaning for your clothes."

"Don't worry about it. Not the first time I've gotten blood on me, won't be the last." He straightened and surprised me by holding out his hand. "We got off on the wrong foot, and that's my fault. I'm sorry, Miss Jones."

Talk about unexpected. I smiled and shook his hand. "Apology accepted."

His return smile looked a bit stiff, but it was probably the first time he'd apologized to a supe. Turning back to Damian, I took a second to think about how easily that word, supe, had come to mind. My day was rapidly approaching "Best Day Ever" status, and it somehow wasn't hard to accept being a supe anymore. I'd been one since the Melding dropped me into a coma.

Part of doing better was accepting who and what I was, and owning it. Still smiling, I said, "Let's get to work."

"Only two items today. After last night, I fully understand if you prefer not to touch either." Damian gestured at the table, where a piece of rope and a bit of scorched gray material waited in evidence bags.

"We have wet wipes and a couple of towels though, just in case," Dodson said.

I didn't look at the two-way mirror, though I could sense the viewing room filling with curious people. Word of last night had spread. "I'm game."

An extra chair was brought in, allowing Dane and Logan to flank me on my side of the table. Since Damian and Dodson didn't sit right next to each other, I was left in full view of the mirror.

The new protocols were becoming habit already, but I made a change when my turn came. "Discord Jones. I'm a natural mage, which is the correct title for people with psychic abilities. I'll be attempting psychometry today."

Damian turned off the recording device, his eyebrows crawling upward. "I thought you didn't like that term?"

Though not cozy with the "children of the gods" association, I shrugged. "I'm okay with it now."

"Alright." He began recording again, letting the guys state their names. "They're both present as support for Miss Jones. Cordi, if you please?"

Hm, rope or cloth first? I chose the rope. Surely, it had had a view of the killer at some point. "The rope."

Dodson slid the evidence bag to me. There were smudges of Mr. Pettigrew stuck to the fibers. I opened the bag, did my abbreviated countdown, and stuck my hand inside.

Bright light and the impression of many people immediately filled my head. "I think it's showing me the store it was in."

Darkness. A rumbling sound. "And now it's in the trunk of a car."

Voices, pressure, and a screeching sound. The rope was being helpful. Mr. Pettigrew's storeroom flashed across my mind, clear for the briefest of instances. "Okay, it was just carried onto the scene, and I heard voices."

"Voices?"

"Yes, definitely more than one. Ooh." My stomach dropped in reaction to a flying sensation. "I'm not seeing anything now, just feeling it. I think the rope was thrown over that beam."

The next sensation was slithering, before weight dragged at the rope. "The victim was just hung."

"Maybe you'd better stop now," Damian said, and I pulled my hand free.

"I didn't see any faces. I didn't see much at all." The feel of something trickling from the top of my head was my first warning. "Not touching doesn't mean that I'm done."

Dane grabbed one of the waiting towels. He put it around my shoulders and pulled my hair out from under it. Liquid slid down my forehead, and scarlet dripped from my left eyebrow, some of it sticking to my eyelashes. I pulled the towel closed in front, noticing that my hands looked fine. "Okay, I..."

Searing pain struck, and I screamed. More blood spilled down, covering my face, and before either shifter could grab hold, I went flying backward and up. My chair thunked to the floor before my back slammed against the wall.

Red and gold and black. *Who'll take care of Rufus?*

That errant thought, whispered in a quavering voice, filled my eyes with tears and momentarily cleared my vision. Logan and Dane were below me, reaching for my dangling hands.

They made contact, the vision ended, and I slid down the wall. My knees buckled when my boots hit the floor, but a quick grab by Logan kept me from going all the way down. "Ow. Am I burned again?"

"Yes, but the bright side is, there's less blood this time," he said.

Raising my head, I grinned, not caring how gory it might look. "It worked."

In the viewing room, someone lost their lunch.

The station had its own small gym in the basement, which meant there were a few showers available. Damian loaned me an STPD T-shirt, because the shoulders of my navy blue sweater were purple from blood that had soaked through the towel.

You'd think another bout of being burned by psychic vision would've dampened my mood, but nope. The only dark spot was that single, clear thought I'd heard: *Who'll take care of Rufus?*

In spite of the agony of his final moments, Mr. Pettigrew's last thought had been worrying about his dog. It saddened me that he'd never know Rufus was safe and okay. The Rottweiler would be, at least to the best of my ability, but I wished there was a way to tell his former owner that.

I rinsed my hair and turned off the water. Maybe there was. It wasn't as though the world lacked magic now. "I'll ask Moira."

"Ask Moira what?" Logan was waiting in the locker room beyond the showers.

"Heh, you caught me talking to myself again." I stuck a hand out to grab the towel waiting on a hook. "Mr. Pettigrew died worrying about Rufus. I'm wondering if there's a way to let him know the dog's being taken care of."

"Have I told you how much I love that you have a good heart?"

"Yes, and then reminded me that hearts are considered a delicacy."

His laugh echoed. "I was a little off that night."

"Yapped your head off. I guess we're even now, huh?" I finished drying and wrapped the towel around my hair. Opening the shower curtain a few inches, I peeked out. "All clear?"

"Yes." Logan had his back to the showers, and his eyes on the door. "She'll be happy to help, if she can."

I slipped out and began to dress. "You know, I thought it might be weird, hanging out with her. I mean, since you two were involved. But it's not."

"She's a hard person to feel uncomfortable around. Good skill for a shaman."

I sat down to put my socks on. "Can I ask you something, since I'm being all mature and adult right now?"

"That's an interesting lead up. Sure."

"Were you in love with her?"

"It's a tricky question to answer, too."

"You don't have to, because it's really not my business. Also, the past is the past."

"I loved her. Still do."

I had an instant need to be fully dressed, but fought it. I picked up my jeans. "Oh."

"Moira was my first, and most serious, past relationship, and she's still a good friend and of course, clan. Part of the reason we didn't work out may have been not being enough in love with her. Not deeply enough for it to last."

I paused before removing the towel from my hair. "I think I get it."

"Good, and I'm glad it doesn't cause a problem between you two. She's a good person to have as a friend." His tone turned teasing. "But if you ever do feel a little jealous, feel free to make it clear that it's you and me now."

I considered throwing the wet towel at his head. "Oh, really?"

"Sure. You know, tiger queens can be pretty possessive when it comes to their men."

"Uh-huh, and just how do they show it?" I pulled on the tee and sat back down to don my boots. They were mid-calf with side zippers.

"Let's just say, they don't have a problem marking their territory."

Did he mean biting? I knew he was teasing me. On the other hand, taking a bite out of him for it sounded like a great idea. Then again, I hadn't noticed any of the clan's men sporting teeth marks— not anywhere visible.

Of course, shifters healed fast. But maybe he meant something else. Puzzling it over, I rose and walked to him. Logan turned around, displaying a devilish grin. "That set your brain on fire."

"You're in trouble. I'm not sure how much yet." My face didn't want to cooperate with my stern tone, and I cracked a smile. "But I think it's a lot."

"I accept any punishment my queen deems fit."

"You never wear pink. Maybe I'll buy you a pink shirt."

He cocked his head. "You can do better than that. Also, not scared of pink. That's a human male issue."

Maybe I should bite his ass. Ooh, I didn't mean his ass, ass but maybe on the neck? Was my face turning red? If it was, could he tell through the layer of blistering? "I'll think of something appropriately dire."

"Quaking in my boots." His grin widened. "Really, I am."

"Oh, shut up." I gave up, and went for serious. "Maybe you haven't you noticed, but I can get a little insecure at times."

Logan immediately sobered. "I will never purposefully give you a reason for jealousy. I won't even tease you about it again."

"I don't mind being teased about anything. I'm just saying that I'll have my dumb moments. Okay?"

"Okay. I'll have mine too. Just tell me. I don't want a communication breakdown between us."

"I don't either, so I'll do my best," I promised, feeling all grown up. Actually, it was getting easier to feel like a real adult, especially with him.

"I promise the same."

We hugged, and I leaned back. "Want to talk about Terra now?"
He winced. "Not yet."

"Okay. Here when you're ready."

Logan kissed me. "Still think I love you."

"Awesome." He must, kissing me while I was covered with gross, little blisters. "We'd better get back upstairs.

TWELVE

"Good lord, Jones. You look like a human-shaped, mushroom pizza." Schumacher tilted his chair back, crossing his hands on his belly. "You ever consider retiring?"

"And forego all this glamorous stuff? Nah." I plopped down in the chair by the side of his desk. "You missed all the fun."

"Heard about it. You made one of the rookies toss his cookies." He waggled his eyebrows and grinned, pleased with his rhyme.

"Well, he was there for a show."

Schumacher boomed out a belly laugh. "They all got more than they bargained for."

"I aim to please. What's up now?"

"Got the run down from the D Squad." He paused, waiting for my reaction.

I grinned. "Better not let them hear you call them that, and don't include me on it."

He chuckled, dropping the front legs of his chair back to the ground. "Now, we're going to have a little chat, see if we can make some more sense of what you saw."

"Sure thing." God, I practically chirped my response. Why was I in such a fantastic mood? Because my "Do Better" resolution was going well, or was it my unintentional soul unburdening to Logan the night before?

Didn't know, and honestly, it didn't really matter. It was awesome to feel so good, mentally and emotionally.

"You saw a store." Schumacher scooped a clipboard off his desk. "Can you remember any distinct details?"

I closed my eyes to bring up the memory, and froze the scene. "Okay, there's a guy in an orange vest who looks like he's helping a customer."

"Good job. I know which home improvement chain that is. Now, can you describe what happened after the," I heard paper rustling. He was checking the clipboard. "The trunk part."

"Sure." I fast-forwarded the memory, slowing it down for the part between the trunk and when my scalp had begun bleeding. Then I replayed it, and again a third time. Opening my eyes, I said, "We're definitely looking for someone with either more than one psychic ability, or more than one person with them. I think at least three."

Schumacher didn't object to my not following his script. "You're determining that from the voices?"

"Yes. Also, I don't think they touched anything at the crime scenes. Not even Mr. Pettigrew. The vision I got from touching his keys, he didn't see them. Wait a sec." I pulled up that memory, and realized I'd missed something. "He did see the rope. He was focused on the door, but I can see the tip of it at the top of his view of the room."

"You're doing great. You're our expert, so put it all together for me, Jones."

I opened my eyes. "They mainly used telekinesis. It's a versatile ability. It was used to break in, to open the safe, the boxes, and on Mr. Pettigrew."

"Why did you end up pinned to the wall?" Dane asked, and I didn't have an answer.

"Not really sure."

Schumacher lifted his hand. "Speaking of, what in the hell is going on with you lately? Spontaneous bleeding, flying out of chairs, and let's not forget you look like a mushroom pizza right now." He put his forefinger and thumb a quarter of an inch apart. "Teensy, weensy mushrooms."

"Physical manifestations of trauma?"

He let the clipboard drop to his desktop. "Plain English, kid."

I fumbled for a better explanation, and hit on one. "I got it: psychic re-enactments, starring yours truly."

The detective sighed. "Maybe you should consider retiring, because that's got to be playing hell with your body."

"Part of the Deluxe Psychic Package." I held my hands up and out, in a "Whatta ya going to do?" gesture. "Back to the point, I think they TKed the rope to snag Mr. Pettigrew. And that means they are pretty damn skilled, so I'm thinking we're definitely looking for vampires."

Schumacher made a "gimme" gesture, and I obliged him. "Only two species get saddled with psychic abilities: humans and vampires. We humans have only had ours for eight years. We haven't had a lot of time to become proficient with them. On the other hand, there are a lot of vamps who have had that time."

"Then it sounds as though a meeting with Lord Derrick is in order."

I turned around in my chair, not having heard Stannett come in. He looked exhausted. "Hi."

"Good to see you, Jones." He greeted Dane and Logan with a quick nod. "Gentlemen."

I checked the time on my phone. It was after one. "Do you want me to call him? He should be awake now."

"Yes, and if you don't mind, can you... what's the word? That thing you did at the school?"

"Teleportation, and no problem. How many people?"

Stannett glanced around. "You four, Herde, Dodson, and me. Is that too many?"

"I can manage." I watched him sit on the corner of Damian's desk, and felt a sneaky vibe from him. He wanted the visit kept quiet. "I'll call him right now."

Derrick actually answered. Did he and Stone share a phone, or what? "Hello, Cordi. What can I do for you today?"

"Hi. First, I'm sorry I only call with questions." That was me, Doing Better.

"You're completely forgiven, if you'll agree to come over tomorrow evening. I'm having a small party." Taken aback, I hesitated, and Derrick smoothly added, "Do bring Logan with you."

"Oh, sure. I mean, if work doesn't prevent it."

"Excellent. Semi-formal attire, and drinks will be served at seven."

"Got it." Partying with vampires. My, how things had changed in just a few short months.

"Now, the reason for your call?"

"We have a situation Chief Stannett would appreciate your input on." I looked at the man, hoping my choice of words was acceptable, and Stannett nodded. Whew.

"I'd be happy to assist in any way possible. When would he like to meet?"

"Now, if that's okay. I'll be providing transportation."

"Discord Airlines." Derrick chuckled. "My library is at your disposal. Have you had lunch yet?"

His chef wasn't the wizard that Thorandryll's was, but still a good cook. Not like I'd pass up a free lunch, anyway. "No, we haven't."

"Then I'll have a luncheon prepared. We'll expect you in the next half-hour."

"Great, we do need to round up a couple of people. There'll be," I silently counted, and half-smiled. "Seven of us."

"Very well. We'll see you shortly."

"Bye." I ended the call. "We're having lunch with Lord Derrick in thirty minutes."

"This ain't a dining room." Schumacher let go of my and Logan's hands. He'd insisted on that spot in our circle, admitting that he was worried about getting "stuck in limbo, or whatever."

"I usually pop in here when they know I'm coming. Front steps when they don't." I had to flex my fingers to encourage blood flow to resume. He'd squeezed too hard.

Dodson was already snooping around the shelves. "Vamps read paranormal romances?"

"I know, right? It's funny." I took a seat on one of the red couches. "I think shifters do too."

"Dane does." Logan sat beside me.

"Hah!" I pointed at our partner, who flushed bright red. "I knew it."

"Shut up." Dane made a face before retreating to the collection of Shakespeare.

"The Bard can't save you now. I know your secret." Man, I could get used to feeling so good. It was nice, even if I wasn't certain of the reason for it.

Stannett wandered around, Damian in tow. Schumacher joined us on the couch. "This is a castle?"

"Pretty much. Not a huge one, but big enough that I wouldn't want to have to clean it."

He grunted. "Me neither. Damian mentioned gargoyles."

"Not here. If you want to meet them, I can ask Petra if it's okay." Crap, I was supposed to visit Tase tomorrow night. I looked at Logan.

Appropriately enough, given our surroundings, he read me like a book. "We'll go by after the party."

"Okay." Problem solved, just like that. Best boyfriend ever.

The library doors opened, turning everyone's head. Stone bowed, straightened, and smiled. "Welcome. We're honored to have you in our home. My master is awaiting us in the dining room, so if you'll please follow me?"

I felt Schumacher shiver. Stone was an impressive sight, but Dodson was just as big. "Come on, folks. No one's going to eat us for lunch."

The dhampyr laughed. "Of course not."

Upon reaching the dining room, I made the introductions while we were seated. The table was shorter than I remembered it being.

Derrick sat at the head, Stone at the foot. I was at the vampire lord's left, Stannett his right. Logan sat beside me, and Schumacher's survival instincts led to him sitting between Logan and Dane. There was an empty chair between Stone and Dodson on the other side of the table, thanks to the odd number of people present.

The meal was served all at once: Juicy pork chops with asparagus and glazed, baby carrots. More of the same waited in covered chafing dishes down the center of the table, if anyone wanted seconds.

After the last servant exited, Derrick gave Stannett his full attention. "I'm eager to learn how I may assist you, but please, don't allow your meal to cool."

Mine wasn't going to get the chance. I dove in, listening to Stannett explain between bites of his own meal. Dodson, his forehead furrowed, was side-eying Stone. The dhampyr was eating with us. It wasn't my place to enlighten the new guy.

In spite of the food, which was good stuff, Stannett managed to complete his explanation by the time I asked Dane to pass the chops for seconds.

He concluded with, "Discretion is required. We don't want to panic people."

"Of course not, and I do appreciate being included." Derrick took a sip from the onyx wineglass before him. I wondered what was in it, not spotting any blood on his lips. "Cordi, would you feel comfortable sharing the visions you had with me?"

"Right now?" I'd just speared a second chop, and held it a little higher, so he'd see.

Derrick's amusement colored his voice. "It'll only take a few seconds, with proper concentration on both our parts."

"I'm kind of not supposed to, because of uh, you know." Mixed company, and some of them didn't need to know that my eyes could change color, or more importantly, that I often felt like munching on humans after contact with a vampire.

"I assure you, it will not be an issue this time." The vampire held out his hand, palm up. "Just concentrate on the visions, and allow me to view them."

Well, shoot. I deposited the pork chop on my plate and put down my fork. Friends weren't truly friends if they didn't trust each other. Derrick and Stone had busted their tails to help find my mom. "Okay."

Placing my hand in his, I discovered his was warm. He'd fed recently, and that was why he was certain Faux Vamp Cordi wouldn't make an appearance.

Yes, it is, Derrick 'pathed, his mental voice calm and soft. The difference from the first time we'd made mental contact was huge. *The visions, if you would?*

I hauled them out from my mental maze for his inspection. Derrick stayed outside the walls, a chilly shadow impression of his physical self.

Thank you. He withdrew from the link and I pulled my hand back. "It does seem clear that vampires are behind these murders. I admit to not understanding why they'd be collecting magical artifacts. It's rare for such objects to respond to us."

"Vamps can't do magic." I picked up my fork and knife. My new pork chop wasn't going to eat itself. "Not the witch or elf kind."

"You could've mentioned that before," Schumacher said. "Please pass the carrots."

"I thought I did mention it."

"No, you said that only humans and vamps get psychically lucky."

I happened to be looking at Damian right then, and the expression on his face was priceless as the warlock stared at his partner. My plate proved less likely to cause giggling. "'Psychically lucky,' really?"

"I thought it sounded nifty. But no, you didn't say 'vampires can't do magic.'" Schumacher ladled a healthy serving of carrots onto his plate.

He hadn't been present at the first scene, when we'd talked about shifters being unable to do magic. And I hadn't said those exact words, when discussing natural magic in regard to vamps. "Okay, I'm sorry. Now you know, and please pass those down when you're done."

"It's possible they're working for hire," Derrick said, ignoring our interruption. "Perhaps collecting the artifacts for a non-vampire employer."

"Do you know how they do the blood thing?" I asked. "The other two abilities are obvious."

"I'm not sure what humans have named it, but we call it 'water calling,' and as you've seen, any type of liquid responds to it. Unfortunately, water calling is the second-most common ability among our people. Telepathy," he inclined his head slightly to me, "being the most common."

"What about pyrokinesis?" That seemed a weird ability for a vampire to have. The older they were, the more combustible.

"Far less common, and that's what we'll focus on during our internal investigation." He returned his attention to Stannett. "If the culprits are part of our community, we will find them. They'll be remanded to your custody."

"Thank you, but I do have to question that 'if.'"

"The council controls the Barrows to the best of its members' abilities, but not all vampires are welcome in our domain. There are others who live above, and of course, there are vampires who prefer to travel from city to city, rather than settling down." Derrick smiled. "Because of that, I'm pleased to offer my son's services. He can act as our liaison, and he's skilled at finding others of our kind."

Schumacher beat Stannett to the question. "Your son?"

"Stone." Derrick's smile widened ever so slightly as he gestured at the other end of the table.

"Ah, some of our work does involve daytime hours."

"Yes, that's why I'm suggesting my son. He's a dhampyr."

"I'm sorry, a what?" Stannett's bewilderment prompted me to answer.

"He's not a full-blown vampire. The sun won't burn him, and he can eat food." I chased a carrot until it was cornered against my pork chop.

"I believe the opportunity to prove we can work together would be invaluable," Derrick said.

Stannett's blood-shot eyes swung my way, and I nodded. "He's trustworthy."

Damian pitched in. "If we're dealing with supernatural perpetrators, it'd be good to have the extra backup, sir."

"All right. I'm not sure the mayor will like the idea, but..."

"Civilian expert," I said pointing at myself. "Vampire expert." I gestured toward Stone.

"That, I can sell." He nodded. "All right. Welcome aboard, Mr. Stone."

"Excellent." Derrick turned and leaned toward me. "I've meant to ask since you arrived. What happened to your skin?"

THIRTEEN

We returned to the station by three-fifteen, with Stone in tow.

"We'll bring Mr. Stone up to speed," Damian said.

"Okay, what do you want us to do?"

"With seven people, I think a division of labor is in order. Someone needs to meet with, ah," Damian whipped out his notebook and riffled through the pages. "Here it is. Meeting with Tanisha..."

Dane interrupted him. "We know her."

"Anything else?" I wasn't going to argue if there was, because I really didn't know how else we could help right now.

"Get a list of the cleaning supplies the museum uses. You can call, text, or email me instead of coming back." Damian smiled, but most of his attention was on Stone. "And we'll call you if anything comes up."

"All right. We have our marching orders, so let's go." I led the way out of the office, slowing down only to tell Stone, "Have fun."

***

"It's just horrible." Tanisha Wills' brown eyes were bloodshot and puffy, but it didn't detract from her looks. Lucky her, because I often thought my photo was next to "ugly cry" in the dictionary. "Ernie was such a sweet man."

We'd offered our condolences upon arrival, which left me with exactly one response. "We'll find who did it. I promise."

She nodded, dabbing at her eyes with a tissue. Taking a deep breath, she managed a small smile. "Reassuring me isn't why you're here though. If you don't mind me asking, why do you look like you were recently burned?"

I didn't want to shove Ernie's brutal passing in her face, so I lied. "It's a weird reaction to an alternative headache remedy."

"Oh, yeah. You've got to be careful with some of that herbal stuff." She nodded. "Okay, the missing artifacts were the Thieves' Stick and the Seven-League Boots."

I glanced at the guys, and neither looked particularly enlightened. "I'm afraid we're not familiar with the fairy tales those are from."

"Supposedly, the stick can be used to open any door, just by tapping the end on one. It didn't work when we tested it." The lovely, dark-skinned woman frowned. "To be perfectly frank, I think a lot of the collection is fake."

Dane had been elected to take notes, because he wrote quickly and the end product didn't look like a couple of hens' scratch-fighting over a worm. His pen began flying over the paper.

"As in, they're all bull crap, or they're substitutes because the owners didn't want to loan out the real thing?" I asked.

"Take your pick. Obviously, the mirror was real, but we haven't seen the spirit since it was returned."

I hadn't noticed the mirror being at the scene the night before. Lady Celadine hadn't informed them the spirit had been relocated. It didn't seem like a good idea to give that information to Tanisha. "Maybe being kidnapped by demons spooked him."

"Could be, and I can't say that I'm sorry it's hiding, but then, you'd have a witness." She dismissed the idea with a wave of her hand. "The boots are allegedly magical transportation, but a code word is required to make them work."

"Betting it's not 'Abracadabra,'" Logan muttered, earning a smile from her.

"Probably not. Of course, we weren't given the code word." Tanisha sniffed. "Being mere mortals, we can't be trusted to resist the lure of magic. We humans are greedy, you know."

I rolled my eyes. "Aren't elves so cool?"

"Oh, absolutely... not." We shared a laugh before she asked, "Is there anything else I can help you with?"

"Yes, please. If you could point us to a maintenance worker? We need a list of the cleaning products you use here."

"Sure. Follow me."

"Okay, all sent." Dane tucked his phone away, and picked his notepad off the trunk of Logan's car. "I forgot to mention that I have a date tonight."

"Ooh, we'd better get him home so he can get beautified for Sheila." I backed away when he tried to muss my hair, and smacked his hand. "No touchee the hair."

"Get in the car, kids." Logan unlocked it. "I can go pick up some dinner after I drop you two off, unless you're wanting to call it a night?"

"I'll cook something for us." Once in the car, I brought up something I'd been thinking about. "Derrick said magical objects don't often work for vamps."

"Yes, he did." Logan backed up the car and changed gears, but he was watching me from the corner of his eye, and there was a hint of a smile curving his lips.

"So would a scent-blocking charm work on them?"

"Good question." Dane leaned forward, blocking our view of each other. "But if the charm doesn't, we have science."

"Huh?"

"Let's assume the perps are definitely doing something to cover their scents, but a magical charm won't do the trick for them. So what's left?"

I drew a blank, and said so. He grinned and sat back. "They could be wearing clothes previously worn by humans. Unwashed clothing."

Logan checked for oncoming traffic before pulling out of the museum's parking lot. "That would cover their scents, especially with the heavy blood odor."

My new thing learned for the day. "Okay, that makes sense."

"They'd have to change right before breaking in, and we know they're fast. It'd take maybe an hour or so for a vampire's scent to saturate the clothing, and overwhelm the human smell." Dane was still grinning. "Like I said, science."

If they both thought that was a possibility, who was I to naysay it? Shifters had better noses. Yet, the New Me felt we shouldn't leave any stones unturned. "Right, but I think I'd like to test whether or not you guys can smell or sense the magic from one of those charms."

"Sure thing. Want me to call David, and ask him if he'll whip up one for us?"

"Please. Tell him we'll come by tomorrow morning." I needed to call Alleryn, not having had a chance to do so yet. For some reason, my phone always managed to find its way to the very bottom of my purse. I dug it out and made the call.

Though thrilled with the news that the guys had again stopped a vision in its tracks, the elf scolded me. "I told you to be careful because we don't know what sort of long-term effects repeated physical manifestations may cause."

"I know, but it's not like I know if one will happen in advance."

Alleryn snorted. "Really? Touching objects involved in brutal murders? I'd think the possibility would be obvious."

"Yes, okay, you're right. But I have to, sometimes." Was I whining? Yes, and Adult Cordi shouldn't be whining like a kid told she had to finish her homework before going outside to play. "I'll try to avoid doing it unless absolutely necessary from now on."

"I suppose that's the best I can hope for. I do recommend that you rest well after an episode."

My reply made Logan chuckle. "I'll go to bed early, Dad."

"Don't get snarky with me, young woman. I'm your doctor," Alleryn shot back. "And your friend."

I tried to sound contrite. "Sorry... Dad."

The elf laughed. "Go home, eat well, and sleep. Doctor Dad's orders."

I ended the call and put my phone away. "I think that's it for our To Do list today."

"Great. We'll have the evening to ourselves." Logan was smiling. "With the dogs."

"*Got it!*" Rufus leaped and caught the ball Logan had thrown. Having skipped my morning jog, I'd decided to kill two birds with one stone: getting some exercise and spending time with my pack. We'd taken a walk first.

The activity was keeping my mind mostly off after-dinner possibilities. My drugged babbling had resulted in a ton of weight lifting off my shoulders, at least in regard to Logan. There was no longer any doubt in my mind that we were serious. It wasn't a rebound thing, and two important items had now been discussed.

Officially, we hadn't been dating long at all, but at least we'd known each other for several months. I still didn't want to rush anything, but the L word *had* come out of both of our mouths this morning. Even with "I think" attached, it was kind of significant.

"Good catch, Diablo." I patted his head when the black pit brought back the ball I'd thrown. "You're getting really good at this."

Tail wagging, he let me take the ball. "*It's fun.*"

Boy, it was awesome to see how far out of his defensive shell Diablo had come. "Ready for another?"

"*Throw it!*" He pranced backward, keeping his eyes on the ball. Laughing, I threw it for him, watching as he turned and raced after it.

Speck clumsily trotted up, his little jaws straining to keep hold of a mini-tennis ball. He dropped it at my feet, looking up with bright eyes. A bit of orange fuzz was stuck to his top lip. "*I carried it.*"

"Just like a big boy." I bent to pet him and picked up the ball. "Want me to throw it for you?"

"*Yes, please.*" His thin tail was a blur.

I tossed it underhanded, in a different direction. The Tinies had the misfortune to be regularly trampled by the larger dogs during games of Fetch. "Go get it."

As Speck bounced off in pursuit of his ball, an argument broke out between Bone and Rufus over whose turn it was to fetch. I took a step toward them, but Logan intervened by pushing between them. "If we can't play nice, fun time is over. It's Bone's turn."

Rufus obediently stepped back and sat down to wait. Logan threw the ball, and after Bone took off, he scratched the Rottweiler behind one ear. "Good boy."

Due to his tail being docked, he couldn't thump like the other dogs, but Rufus wiggled at the praise, his stump wagging. Satisfied the situation was resolved, I looked around for Squishy, who was barking.

Leglin was keeping her occupied by holding a tug o' war rope, the end dangling low enough for her to reach. As I watched, she grabbed it and shook her head then let go to bark again. Rinse, and repeat. Diablo loped back, and I had to get busy throwing balls again.

Roughly an hour passed before I called a halt to the festivities. "I need to start some dinner if we want to eat tonight." A chorus of doggy protests filled the air. "Sorry, but it's getting dark, too, and I'm cold."

"*Wuss,*" Bone mumbled around the ball.

I pointed at him. "So nice of you to volunteer to pick up the toys tonight."

"*Not fair!*"

"*I'll help,*" Rufus said. "*We put them in the basket?*"

Bone dropped the ball to lick the Rottie's face. "*Yeah. Thanks.*"

"They'll pick up," I told Logan, happy the two were over their fussing, and that Rufus was so eager to fit in. "I'm going in to wash up."

"Okay, I'll bring in the basket when they're done, and make sure everyone comes inside."

"Thanks." I stopped in passing to kiss him, resulting in that weird little tingling, and went inside, wondering what exactly caused it.

FOURTEEN

That infrequent, unexplained tingling occupied my thoughts as I washed my hands and scouted the fridge and pantry for dinner possibilities. Pickings were slim, reminding me that I needed to hit the grocery store soon, but I figured something out.

Tingles didn't strike every single time Logan and I touched, and they hadn't happened just with him. I'd felt them a few times in contact with Thorandryll, and didn't that beat all?

I'd never felt them with Nick, or when in contact with any other shifter or elf. This wasn't the first time I'd puzzled over them, and I had previously decided they weren't sexual in nature, because they didn't last very long.

However, the real question was whether or not they were important, and it wasn't a question I could answer alone. "I should ask Logan if he feels them. Maybe we can figure out what's causing them together."

Together. A goofy feeling smile spread across my face as I cut up boneless chicken breasts and put them on to boil in broth. Based on our morning talk, we were on the same page, and would be doing a lot of things together from now on.

I chopped up a handful of carrots, dumping them and a cup of frozen peas into the pot. Next up: mixing the ingredients for the dumplings. The front door opened then, a stream of dogs preceding Logan. I counted heads, and everyone was present.

He left the basket by the coatrack, and hung up his jacket before coming to the kitchen. "What are we having?"

"Chicken and dumplings."

"Do you need any help?"

"Nope, I've got it under control, but if you wouldn't mind feeding them?" I jerked my chin at the furry puddle at the end of the breakfast bar.

"No problem." He went to the pantry. Everyone knew where the dog food and bowls were kept, if they'd hung out with me for longer than a day.

"I have a question."

"Shoot."

"Have you ever," I paused to check my milk measuring. "Felt a shock or tingling when we touch?"

"There was that one time, but I think that was a socks and carpet thing."

I threw a potholder at him. Logan caught it without looking up from doling out dogfood into bowls.

"Come on, it's a serious question."

"All right." He tossed the potholder on the breakfast bar's counter. "I certainly feel things when we touch, but a shock hasn't been one of them."

The urge to go off-track was strong, in order to explore exactly what kind of things he felt. But only for a second. We could discuss that later, maybe after dinner. "How about tingling?"

A slow smile appeared on his face as Logan put the dogfood away. "Occasionally, yes." He began placing the bowls on the floor, stretching them out from the end of the kitchen into the hallway. "But I'm not sure if we're talking the same kind."

We were definitely going to discuss that later, and in depth, too. "Can I show you what I mean?"

"Sure, give me a sec." He finished his task, and went to the sink to wash his hands. "Okay."

Dumplings mixed, I recalled every instance that I could of feeling those particular tingles before holding out my right hand. He took hold with his, as though we were about to shake hands. Establishing a telepathic link with him had never been difficult, almost as though one were always present between us.

Watching his face, I transferred those remembered instances to him. He blinked, his forehead furrowing. "Okay, not the same type of tingles."

Ooh. "All righty then. Now, don't be offended, please, but I should tell you that I never felt those with Nick. On the other hand," I sent him the few instances the tingles had occurred while I was in contact with Thorandryll.

"Huh," was his first reaction, and his second was, "Why would that offend me?"

"I don't know." Silly me, forgetting he didn't have a fragile ego. "It's weird, right?"

He nodded, his thumb caressing the back of my hand. I think he meant it to be reassuring, but instead, the gesture caused tingles of an entirely different variety from the ones we were discussing. "A little strange, yeah. No idea what they may mean?"

"Nope. I need to check on the chicken."

Logan released my hand, moving to lean against the counter so we could still see each other while talking. "Maybe we should run some tests."

"What kind of tests?"

"Fun ones." He waggled his eyebrows, following up with a big grin.

"I will throw another potholder at you." A smile ruined my threat. "You've been flirty today, mister."

"I didn't tell you everything you said last night. Or for that matter, everything you did."

Oh, great. It sucked not knowing what he was talking about, and I could only imagine what drugged, blabbermouth Cordi may have done after our morning discussion. "Please tell me that I didn't..."

"Do your best to sweet talk me out of my pants?" Logan gave a single nod, crossing his arms and trying to look stern. "Oh, but you did. You were really determined. I barely escaped with my virtue intact."

Oh, God. Was he teasing me again? I studied his expression. Nope, he was serious. "I hope I only talked."

"You mostly talked." When I cringed, he relented, beginning to smile. "I'm exaggerating a little. You didn't cross any lines."

His lines, or mine? No meant no, and it sounded like I'd tried to wheedle a yes out of him. I owed him an apology. "I am so sorry for being such a jerk last night."

Logan's smile faded. "You weren't a jerk. Even under the influence, you were still you. Not some stranger. Okay, yeah, the rap part was kind of out there on the fringes, and surprised me."

It was time to begin adding the dumplings. I retrieved the bowl and started dropping spoonsfull of dough into the bubbling pot. "I'll tell you a secret."

Uncrossing his arms, Logan half-turned and dramatically braced on the countertop. "I'm ready."

"Ginger and I used to have cussing contests. I think when we were about eleven."

"Based on last night, I'm going to guess you usually won those contests." He relaxed, leaning his hip against the counter.

"Yep, and you can thank my mom for that."

Logan's chin dipped, his eyes widening. "Sunny? No way."

"Yes way. You've never seen her truly pissed off, and when she totally loses the 'peace and love' vibe. It's a sight to behold, and I promise, your ears burn for days afterward."

He was still laughing when I finished adding the dumplings.

The after-dinner plan was a movie, but ten minutes in, a friendly wrestling match over one of the throw pillows led to a makeup kiss. One kiss led to another, until we were making out like a couple of teenagers.

Logan's shirt went first, mine following two or three kisses later. Legs tangled with his, and deep in the middle of a sweet, slow kiss, with his fingers tracing skin-shivering designs on my back, I realized the ringing phone wasn't part of the movie. It was the regular ring, not any of the ringtones I'd assigned my friends or family.

I interrupted our lip lock just long enough to say, "I'm not answering it."

"Okay." His eyes were caught between pine green and gold, and he was breathing as hard as I was. Diving into another kiss, we both groaned when his phone began to ring too. He quietly growled as our kiss broke, but said, "Maybe we'd better answer them."

Damn it. "I guess so."

Somehow, we managed to untangle without falling off the couch. I had to head to the dining area to retrieve my phone. Logan's was on the coffee table, and I listened as he answered it. "Hello? What? No, I'm at her place."

My phone stopped ringing. I checked the display, and didn't recognize the number. Going back to the couch, I picked our shirts up off the floor.

"We're on our way," Logan said, his eyebrows drawing down. Ending the call, he took his shirt. "They struck again."

"Where?"

"Thorandryll's." He began pulling his shirt on as my jaw dropped.

"They hit an elf's house?"

"Yeah, and killed one."

"Holy crap." I couldn't comprehend the news. "How did they get in?"

"I guess we'll find out." He ran a hand through his hair, drawing in a deep breath. I yanked on my shirt—or actually, Damian's because I hadn't changed since arriving home—while he slowly exhaled. His eyes were dark again when he finished, the golden flecks hidden because the only light was from the TV. "Not exactly how I was hoping the night would end."

Me neither, and I had the feeling we wouldn't be feeling amorous later. But there was tomorrow, and then next day, and the one after that... "Rain check?"

Logan smiled, bending to grab his boots. "Definitely."

"We'll teleport." It'd save time, and since Thorandryll liked summertime, we wouldn't even need our jackets.

"Sounds like a plan. Do you want to drop the dogs off at my place? I have an extra bedroom now. In fact, why don't you grab whatever you need, and just stay over there tonight?"

It occurred to me that he'd gotten used to having Terra there, and wasn't enjoying the abrupt change. "Sure, I'll be a couple of minutes."

Trotting upstairs, I wondered how the hell vampires had gotten into Thorandryll's sidhe without being detected right off the bat. The place was riddled with both elves and magic. No answer came to mind as I packed.

Back downstairs, I discovered he'd gathered the dogs' lounging pillows together. Speck and Squishy peered out from under a throw on the uppermost one. Logan picked up the soft tower, carefully balancing the whole pile. "We're ready."

"I see that. Okay, everyone close and touching." Bone and Diablo pressed Rufus between them. I hooked a finger in Logan's belt, and touched Leglin's neck. My hound dropped his muzzle to Bone's back. "And away we go."

FIFTEEN

About ten minutes later, I was regretting my decision to appear unannounced on the wrong side of Thorandryll's front doors. We raised our arms, facing a trio of elves with bows pointed at us. "Here to help, don't shoot."

They lowered their weapons in unison, and one stepped forward. "My apologies, Lady Discord. We're on high alert, after this evening's event."

I recognized him. "No harm done, Edrel. Where do we go?"

"You'll need an escort. A moment." He whipped out a cell phone from somewhere, possibly thin air. Within seconds, he'd made a call and was speaking to whoever it was. "Sir, Lady Discord has arrived. Of course."

Whisking the phone back out of sight, Edrel smiled. "Lord Kethyrdryll is on his way."

"Thank you." There was a bench seat, upholstered in pale green linen, against one wall. I didn't remember it from previous visits. "Is it okay if we sit down?"

"Certainly." As we walked over and sat, one of the other elves said something in Elvish with a faint sneer on his face. He was watching Logan closely. Edrel replied in the same language, his tone sharp. A heated exchange commenced, the third elf silently distancing himself from them by a few steps.

"Is there a problem?" I finally asked.

Edrel began to shake his head, but the other elf, a slender guy with midnight hair, narrowed his nearly silver eyes at me. "You dishonor the prince, consorting with animals."

Pre-Do Better Me wanted to sling him into the opposite wall, sneer first. Post-Do Better Me suggested that may be a bad idea, under the circumstances, what with two other armed elves as an audience. So I smiled, finding Logan's hand without looking, and laced our fingers together. "We've never met, have we?"

"No." Midnight's sneer deepened.

"Didn't think so, or you'd know that you're speaking to a clan queen."

"You sound as though you are proud of that title."

"Because I am." I lifted my chin, keeping my eyes on his. "And I don't appreciate my people being insulted."

"Apologize," Edrel ordered, practically hissing the word out.

"I will not."

The third elf, who had brown hair liberally streaked with dark green, chose to speak up. "Our Prince holds Lady Discord in high regard. He will not be pleased to learn you have insulted her."

"Or Logan." I leaned slightly forward, lowering my voice. "You know, not so long ago, Thorandryll told me he respects Logan."

Surprise fluttered from Logan, and his fingers twitched.

"Lord Kethyrdryll calls this shifter friend," the third elf quietly added. "I have heard him do so."

Midnight's sneer had faded, but he held onto his natural arrogance. Bowing with an overdone flourish, he said, "It appears I've misspoken. My apologies."

If I'd slammed him into the wall, we wouldn't have gotten an apology. Okay, he obviously wasn't sincere, but still. He'd apologized. "Accepted."

Kethyrdryll came striding down the hall, and halted a few feet away to survey us. He frowned. "Is there something amiss?"

"Nope, we were just having a friendly chat." I stood, Logan shadowing me, and walked over to the new arrival. "It's good to see you again, in spite of the circumstances."

"We must arrange a social visit." Kethyrdryll smiled, taking my hand when I extended it. After touching his lips to my knuckles, he released me and turned to Logan. "Well met, my friend."

I couldn't resist looking over my shoulder to give Midnight a saccharine smile. The black-haired elf looked like he'd just sucked on a lemon, his lips pursed and tight. *Hah, put that in your pipe and smoke it, buddy.*

"Well met, Lord Kethyrdryll." They did the warrior's grip thing, genuine warmth emanating from Logan. Kethyrdryll was the only elf we'd met who didn't act like shifters were something nasty he'd managed to step in.

"They're expecting us, so we should be on our way."

We followed him down the hall. I couldn't keep from looking around, wondering if the place had gotten bigger. There seemed to be a lot more doors down each wall, and... where the hell had that staircase come from? It was a one-story building, wasn't it? High-ceilinged rooms, but still one-story. My brain twitched. *Pocket realm, girl. Let it go.*

"It was Jeharin," Kethyrdryll said. "The man we lost."

My boots were the only ones squeaking on the marble floor. How did elves and shifters move so damn quietly? "We're sorry for your loss."

Logan's hand slipped back around mine, and we exchanged tiny smiles as the elf responded. Our cutesiness should've made me want to gag, but didn't.

"Thank you. You met him. The silver-haired lad who accompanied my brother on the mission to rescue you?"

I took a few steps before recalling the guy. He'd agreed with my idea about carrying people bits before we entered the maze, but we'd never talked beyond that. "I remember him. He seemed nice."

"A highly skilled warrior, yet, they overpowered him." Shaking his head, the elf opened a door on the left. "Through here."

I balked, not looking inside. "The scene's right there?"

"No," Logan answered, giving my hand a light tug. "She'll need a minute before seeing Jeharin's remains."

"Of course. We'll halt before the corridors intersect." Kethyrdryll went through the doorway, and we followed. My sense of space was taking a serious beating, because it felt like we walked farther than the outer walls would allow, before reaching steps leading down.

Logan broke the silence as we began descending. "Something's bothering me."

"What?"

"They broke into a pocket realm, where the sun can appear in an instant. That strikes me as really risky for vampires."

Which reminded me... "Hey, Kethyrdryll, do you know anything about scent-blocking charms? Specifically, do they work on vampires?"

"That would depend on the skill of the practitioner. I could create a charm to mask a vampire's scent, if the vampire who'd be wearing it was present." He paused upon reaching the bottom of the stairs.

"They won't work if not customized?" Maybe science was the answer then.

"Vampires live, but are not alive in the same fashion as we are. That difference prevents them from," the elf hesitated. "It's rather complex, actually. They're rarely able to use magic other than natural magic, as you do. Fascinating, because vampires existed outside the natural order. The dead should not walk."

An irrational urge to defend vamps rose, but I ignored it. It wasn't pertinent. "Ronnie can make wards that keep vampires out."

Kethyrdryll nodded, gesturing for us to keep moving. "Yes, magic can be used against them effectively, whether natural or other forms. As I mentioned, it's a complex subject."

Not too long ago, he'd explained magic to me in simple terms. "You told me that magic is energy, and that people access it in different ways."

"And with varying degrees of competency, yes."

"Right. If vampires are outside the natural order, how can they use any magic at all, much less 'natural' magic?"

A gleam appeared in the elf's eyes, and his tone became enthusiastic. "My personal theory is that the change from living to death to undead is so abrupt, their sparks of magic aren't shed."

"I think you need to back up a little. Sparks of magic?"

"Every living thing has at least a drop of the energy we call magic. The majority of living things can't access that drop, or spark. It's too small and weak," he said.

"Okay." I let that settle for a few seconds. "Does that mean I have more drops than say, Damian?"

"Yes. Your magic is an ocean compared to his puddle. Or for different imagery, you have a boulder of magic, while he has a pebble."

My forehead was wrinkling. "How can I have so much magic, yet my parents don't have any? Or I guess, they only have sparks?"

"That is a matter of... what is the word?" He rubbed his chin, his eyes briefly narrowing. "Oh, genetics."

Hello, science territory. I hoped he kept things simple. "I don't think I get it."

"A child is the sum of combined genetic material from two parents. Not all of that genetic material is active, and some that is active is suppressed due to one parent's genes being more dominant." Kethyrdryll glanced at me, and I nodded to let him know I was following along.

"I believe it's entirely possible that centuries of inactive or suppressed—no, that's not the correct word, what is it? Oh—recessive genetic material passed along will become active or dominant under the right circumstances."

Logan asked the question I was beginning to put together to ask myself. "Who's capable of manipulating things to make sure the right circumstances occur?"

"Well, Nature of course, and I suppose the gods as well. After all, they are the purest expression of magic in the world."

My scalp prickled, and goosebumps broke out on my arms. "Petra told me that she thinks I'm the product of an intensive breeding program, because of the," I paused, trying to recall her exact words. "The lack of dilution in my bloodline. She doesn't think it's a coincidence I have so many abilities, considering the passage of time from Sundering to Melding."

"Ah." The elf sobered. "I see."

"Back to the subject, that means gods are at the top of the magical food chain. Natural mages are second?"

"As far as being conduits for magic, yes. In practice, age and experience do matter."

"Right." That probably meant overall, elves were in second place, and would be for a while. Vamps or mages in third? I didn't have time to ask, because the low murmur of voices reached us.

"It's just ahead to the left," Kethyrdryll said.

"Thanks for the warning."

The wall around the vault, and the door of it, had borne the brunt of Jeharin's death. His body had been completely vaporized, no partial corpse, or even recognizable bits, left.

For some reason, that made not throwing up easier, though I was beginning to wonder if I'd ever get rid of the charnel stench in my nasal passages.

Gloves on and shoes covered, I took advantage of everyone being busy to teleport into the open vault. No sense tracking through elf goop if I didn't have to. To my disappointment, there wasn't much to see.

The vault's interior was a long space maybe fifteen feet wide. I couldn't estimate how long, because I couldn't see the far end. Both walls were covered in metal doors in a variety of sizes. Safety deposit boxes for magical objects.

Only one was open, or rather, its little door had been forced opened, leaving it hanging by the bottom hinge.

"Curiosity killed the cat, Miss Jones."

I jumped and uttered a squeak, turning wide eyes on Thorandryll. Jaws clenched and icy blue peepers narrowed, he appeared ready to murder somebody. Wasn't going to be me. "My sympathies on your loss."

His face tightened and then his expression softened. "Thank you."

Already back to studying the open deposit box, I asked, "What was in here?"

"Your tendency to focus on business is often annoying."

I just looked at him. Seriously, what did he expect? For me to start weeping and pulling out my hair? Or perhaps for me to embrace him, smooshing his face into my breasts, all the better to comfort him as he wept small, manly tears?

"Very well." Thorandryll sighed. "A ring with the power to mesmerize any living being."

Hm. "Doesn't work, does it?"

"*Au contraire*, my skeptical lady. It does work, if one knows the proper word to use it."

Turning to him, I smiled. "And you don't."

Up went his left eyebrow. "Why would you think that?"

Because he would've used it on me. A mesmerized Cordi was a married-to-an-elf-prince-and-under-control Cordi. "Do you really want me to answer that?"

"Your low opinion of me is quite wounding, Miss Jones." His smirk said something way different than his words.

Rolling my eyes, I turned my back to him in order to look down the vault room. "Are you certain that's all they stole?"

"Yes."

All those doors, hiding away who knew what, and he'd pitched a hissy fit over my destroying one measly grimoire? What a greedy little elf. "If I find your ring and learn the right code word, I'm not telling you what it is. Just sayin'."

His laughter rang and echoed, rolling away from us in gradually softer repeats. "I'd expect nothing less. Though should you ever tire of being in Lord Whitehaven's employ, I believe you'd discover solving such minor mysteries to be extremely lucrative."

Maybe he couldn't use most of what he had hidden down here. In fact, maybe a lot of people couldn't use the magical artifacts they had, if the common failsafe was designing them to be used with code words. I liked that thought a lot. "I'll keep that in mind."

"Obtaining hard-to-locate items would be another option."

I snorted. "I'm not going Dark Side to steal stuff for you."

More laughter from him. I shook my head and went to the vault's entrance, to see what was going on in the corridor.

SIXTEEN

As it turned out, not much was going on. Photos were still being shot, and evidence collection was underway. Not that there'd be much to collect. My team members stood together on the other side of the splatter and smear area. Looking at them, I realized only Damian and Stone stood with Logan. No Dodson or Schumacher. Damian was the shortest of the three men, and possibly, the shortest supe present. I doubted it bothered him.

I teleported over, again avoiding elf goop, and turned to look at the door. It was metal, more than a foot thick, and there wasn't an obvious handle or locking mechanism. However, it had been wrenched out of true, the top angled slightly forward. "I guess magic locking spells don't hold their own against telekinesis."

"No," Damian agreed. "Doesn't look that way.

"Where's Dodson?" I knew where Dane was, and guessed Schumacher was out by the cars, or had begged off on this one. He seemed to be losing his stomach for the results of supernatural murder, and I couldn't blame him. I'd never really had the stomach for it.

"Anniversary dinner for his parents. Schumacher had already left for the day, but Mr. Stone was still there."

Lucky them, getting to skip this mess. I exchanged a nod with the dhampyr, who stood at the warlock's left shoulder. Either Damian didn't care Stone was in his personal bubble, or he was too preoccupied to realize it. "What do you want me to do?"

"Are you up to touching the victim's weapons?"

I took another look at the mess, and saw a sword and bow off to the right of vault's opening. Both were liberally covered in elf goop. "If they're cleaned off first, sure."

Damian nodded, his eyes moving over the scene. I wondered if he was committing it to memory, or maybe, looking for something beyond the obvious. "I'll make the request."

Kethyrdryll was standing a few feet away, and cleared his throat. "I'll see to it."

"Thank you." The warlock continued to visually rake over the scene. "Something's not adding up for me. It's like we're missing a puzzle piece, but it's on the table in front of us."

"Actual motive and viable suspects to hunt down?" I crossed my arms, watching Thorandryll exit the vault. He used the somewhat clearer path the door's forced opening had made in the mess.

His shiny black boots looked silly with shoe coverings, and I regretted missing how he'd taken being told he had to wear those and gloves. Reaching us, he began peeling off the gloves. "When will your people be finished?"

"Another hour or so, sir."

"Good. We need to gather as much of our fallen warrior's remains as possible, to properly lay him to rest." The prince focused on me. "It slipped my mind earlier, but we need to schedule a meeting, Miss Jones."

"Why?"

"A small matter, though perhaps not one to discuss publicly."

Now what in the hell was he talking about? I wracked my brain, but the only thing that came up was our becoming officially allied. "Sure. How about four tomorrow?"

"Acceptable."

I hoped it wouldn't take long, because I'd need time to get ready for Derrick's party. "I'll let you know if I can't make it for some reason."

A couple of elves in gray uniforms arrived, pushing a cart holding buckets and cloths. Thorandryll frowned. "The police aren't done here."

"I called for them. The detective has asked Lady Discord to handle Jeharin's weapons," Kethyrdryll said. "She prefers to do so after they've been cleaned."

"My permission was not..."

I interrupted him before his snootiness got the better of him. "We're hoping they saw the killers."

"Ah. Very well, you may proceed." Thorandryll gave his Royal Nod.

"So gracious of you, Your Highness." The sarcasm dripping from my voice didn't escape his notice, earning me a glare. I suddenly wondered if I could take him, should we ever go toe to toe magically.

No lie, it'd be pretty satisfying to rub his nose in the dirt a few times. But not exactly beneficial to my future, either personally or professionally. After all, Thorandryll could be mayor one day. I gave that slim odds, but it could happen.

Thorandryll's glare had become a thoughtful gaze, and I realized the others were watching us stare at each other. *Ack.*

I broke eye contact and looked at Logan, who had a faint smile on his face. I hoped he didn't think I'd been fantasizing about the elf. Okay, I kind of had been, but not in the sexy way. "Will you need us after I've done that?"

Damian startled, and pulled his eyes from the mess to look at me. "Only if anything useful results."

"Cross your fingers." The two servants were washing the sword first. I glanced around the scene before asking, "Jeharin wasn't wearing armor?"

"I seldom require my internal security to wear it." Thorandryll scowled. "It wouldn't have made a difference."

Probably not, but a hunk of shiny metal facing the killers could've been useful. My eyes wandered in Stone's direction. "What kind of warding do you have?"

The prince didn't look at the dhampyr. "The warding worked. An alarm sounded. Unfortunately, the filthy little bastards acted too quickly, and were gone before reinforcements arrived."

"I see. Better add teleportation to the list of the killers' abilities." Elves could teleport too, but it wasn't quite the same thing I did. They sort of... melted between places. It wasn't instantaneous like my ability, but took a second or two.

Damian had his notebook out, adding the note. Stone cleared his throat. "That's another rarity among our people."

Good to know. "Might want to update Derrick then."

He pulled out his cell phone and asked Damian, "If I may?"

"Go right ahead."

"Did an alarm sound when they arrived?" I flipped my hand at the two.

"No. They came openly, through the front gates."

Hm. "Does one sound when I pop in?"

Thorandryll smiled, not answering. Freaking elf. Oh, but wait. The first time I'd popped in without an invitation—albeit by accident—Logan and I had been surrounded by armed elves. But none had appeared the next day, when I popped in to collect belongings we'd left behind. And none had appeared the day I popped in to talk to him, okay, kind of blackmail him, about Leglin.

Seemed to indicate he'd tweaked his wards or something, to allow me free passage. Yet, that didn't mean his sidhe wasn't somehow signaling him when I arrived. Just him, not everyone.

I smiled back, realizing I may have just solved the minor mystery of there always being the right number of chairs when I came visiting. Logan could probably confirm my theory, having helped design the clan's pocket realm. "Sneaky."

"It's fascinating to watch you think, Miss Jones."

"I'll work on my poker face." The sword was clean. Skirting the Jeharin Explosion, one of the servants carried it to me and dropped to one knee. He bowed his head before looking up, the sword lying flat across his raised palms. "My lady."

I wasn't his lady, or his prince's, but arguing over the form of address had proven futile in the past. "Thank you, but you'd better hand it to someone else. Damian's not ready."

The servant blinked, his pale lilac eyes moving to Thorandryll. I realized he was just a boy, maybe sixteen or seventeen. Most elves seemed frozen somewhere between twenty-five and thirty, so he was the first teenager I'd seen.

"Your Highness?" The kid's voice quavered.

"Good of you to notice," Thorandryll said, his lips flattening into a thin line.

The sword-bearer flinched, the tips of his ears turning pink. "M-my apologies, Your Highness."

Oh, he'd screwed up, speaking to me first. I had the feeling a scathing reprimand was on the way, and did my best to divert Thorandryll. "Get your phone ready, Damian."

"Just a sec."

Both elves looked at me, the teen with open-mouthed surprise. Guess no one dared to interrupt when Thorandryll was in a mood. "New protocols. We have to video when I use psychometry on police cases."

"For what reason?" The prince's brows drew together, but at least he wasn't glaring the kid into a puddle of submission.

"Chain of evidence." Damian moved closer, fiddling with his phone. "And it'll prevent Cordi from having to appear in court as much."

I actually didn't go to court often, but kept my mouth shut. By the time a police case was closed, there was usually enough evidence that having a psychic appear was overkill.

"I see." And Thorandryll didn't like it, judging by his scowl. I wondered why, since the jerk hadn't had a problem parading me before cameras not quite two weeks prior.

"Okay, I'm ready." Damian held up his phone. "If you would?"

"Discord Jones, natural mage." I didn't miss the prince's tiny startle. "I'm going to use psychometry on this sword and a bow. One, two, three."

Placing my hand on the sword, I received a quick response. A thrill of rage clenched my teeth, drawing my lips back into a silent snarl. The elf teen's eyes widened, white showing all the way around his irises. I jerked my hand back. "Whoa. It's mad. Really, really mad."

"The emotion is Jeharin's, yes?" Thorandryll edged into my personal bubble.

"Well, yeah. Inanimate objects don't have emotions. They're like batteries." I needed to touch the sword again, and hoped it would offer something less rage-fueled, and more useful. "I'm going to try again."

My second attempt wasn't exactly productive either. A feeling of surprise, darkness becoming light, and nothing else. "They surprised him, but we already knew that."

About to lift my hand, I paused when an image of me appeared. Not the me currently touching the sword, but a me standing next to a huge black tiger, surrounded by snow. Voices whispered, but I couldn't make out the words.

Strange. Why would we make such an impression on Jeharin that he retained that memory and passed it into his sword?

"Anything else?" Damian asked, and I shook my head while moving my hand.

"Nothing relevant to the case. Just a memory of snow."

He stopped recording. "Do you think it's necessary to try the bow?"

Not really, since it appeared the sword had been Jeharin's weapon of choice when the intruders appeared. Yet, I was curious what his bow might show me. "Let's be thorough."

"Right."

The other servant brought the bow, and kneeling beside the teen, and did the head duck while offering the weapon. "Your Highness, Lady Discord."

"Thank you. Ready, Damian?"

He lifted his phone again. "Go ahead."

Since I'd already mentioned the bow, I didn't reintroduce myself. Counting down, I placed my hand on the smooth, reddish wood.

Past Me, rising from the celebratory banquet and bumping Logan. Logan disappearing into my room in the pavilion. Me, going into the same room.

Jeharin had certainly kept his eye on us. Why?

Nothing else showed. I shrugged, and dropped my hand. "No go."

"Damn, all right." Damian put his phone away. "I guess that's it then."

We could go, woohoo. "Any idea if you'll need us tomorrow?"

"Not unless something comes up. I'll let you know, or you let me know. Thanks, Cordi."

"You're welcome." I took a step away from them, toward Logan, and froze as a tracking thread unfurled. "I have a trail."

"Let's move."

The thread was multicolored, but what worried me more was the way it was pulsing. "I don't think it's going to last long."

I took off at a run, not waiting to see if they followed. Down the intersecting corridor, up the stairs, back through the too long hallway, and out into the great hall. From their positon at the front door, Edrel and the other two guards spun around, bows rising. They instantly dipped again. I threw them a wave, following the thread that had turned into another doorway.

It was the ballroom, and I tripped going down the first few steps. Catching my balance, I made it down the rest without trouble. The thread went straight to the double doors leading outside. I broke a nail opening them, being in such a hurry. "Ouch, damn it."

It wasn't bleeding, and I charged outside, shaking away the sting. The others were following, maybe twenty feet behind. The thread kept going, through and out the garden, across the lawn, and into the trees. I had to slow down to avoid low hanging branches and stealth twigs determined to put my eyes out.

The thread's pulsing began to slow, and with each, the thread grew less visible. "Crap."

I picked up the pace again, holding my arms up and out, to protect my face. Ten steps later, I ran into something and was knocked on my ass. "Oof."

The thread disappeared, and I thought I heard a feminine giggle just before everyone caught up. Logan dropped to his knee beside me, his hand going to my back. "What happened? Are you okay?"

"Yeah." I stared at the space before me, my hands and forearms stinging, wondering what the hell I'd run into. There was nothing there, between the two trees. "And I don't know. My trail's gone."

SEVENTEEN

Teeth brushed, face washed, and PJs on, I left the bathroom still puzzling over the invisible barrier I'd struck. It was gone when we checked, but the men had been close enough to witness me running into it.

Well, those with excellent night vision had, which meant Logan, Stone, and the royal twins. Damian and the uniformed officer he'd tagged to go hadn't.

And no one else had heard the giggle.

Logan was in the kitchen, watching coffee brew. I paused in the doorway, because he'd changed into a pair of blue and green plaid sleep pants. The view was really nice.

"I like your new kitchen." I walked in, sliding a finger over the closest dark green and white marble countertop. Smatterings of brown and flecks of gold were present in the marble too. The cabinets were a smoky, golden wood. "It's bigger than my kitchen."

He grinned. "I had you in mind when designing it."

"Oh?"

"Figured a big, pretty kitchen might result in being offered cooking lessons."

"Uh huh." I patted the countertop, ticking off the kitchen's features in my mind. The appliances were black: a double oven stove, dishwasher, and a nice, French door fridge. Plenty of prep space available. The double sink was some dark green material, and deep. "When did you want to start those lessons?"

"How about in the morning?" Logan opened a top cabinet and pulled out two mugs.

"Sure." I crossed to stand closer while he poured the coffee. My hands were itching to explore his back. Not like they hadn't earlier, but we'd been interrupted.

He moved, retrieving a carton of half and half from the fridge. "You're staring."

"I am. There's a sexy, half-dressed man making me coffee in a beautiful kitchen."

Lips quirked, he asked, "Which is the bigger draw, the kitchen or me?"

"Ooh, tough call." I held my hand up, thumb and forefinger slightly apart. "You win by this much."

Logan laughed, and added sugar to one mug before handing it to me. "I apparently did too good of a job on this kitchen."

After a sip, I said, "You did a great job on my coffee too. Thanks."

"Welcome." He put the half and half away, coming back to pick up his mug. "Wondering something."

"What?"

"What were you thinking when you and Thorandryll were having that stare off?" He leaned his hip against the counter. I rested mine too, on the other side of the sink from him.

"I was wondering something too: Whether or not I could kick his ass, if we ever have a throw down."

"Physically, no. I might be able to, if I surprised him and got the upper hand quickly." Logan hesitated. "You have good reflexes and can think fast under pressure."

"There's a but coming up, isn't there?" I didn't mind, too busy watching his face, particularly the way his lips moved as he talked.

"Well, yeah, and I hope it doesn't piss you off." He took a drink of coffee, waiting for me to respond.

"You two grew up in the same world. I grew up in this one. Tell me the but."

"Okay. But, he's over two thousand years old. That means he's had a lot of time to build magical muscle memory."

I nodded. "You're right."

"Whew." Logan mimed wiping sweat off his forehead and grinned. Did I react that badly to people offering constructive criticism? "You can build magical muscle memory too. But you'll need to practice a lot, do some technique refining."

"Yeah, and find a private place to practice, where there's no danger to anyone or anything if I mess up."

He threw out his free arm. "You're standing in it."

"Your kitchen?"

"No, silly woman. We live in a pocket realm, remember?"

"Yeah, but..."

Logan dropped his arm. "There's a meadow a mile and half or so north of here. It's roughly two acres, and a nearly perfect oval. We can put a thick, high stone wall around it, and ta-dah! You'll have a safe, private practice arena."

"Wow." I couldn't believe he'd offer me something like that.

His grin reappeared. "Good idea, huh?"

"It's a fantastic idea, but would doing it upset anyone?"

"A few deer, but they can be directed to another meadow," He assured me. "We can go take a look tomorrow."

I hesitated, but knew I really needed such a place. "Okay."

"Oh, and at some point, we need to make an appointment with Kiffle."

"Who?"

Logan lifted his mug in an abbreviated salute. "I promised you armor. He's the best armorer I know."

Oh, he'd remembered. How sweet! "I was kidding, Logan. You don't have to," I stopped when he lifted his hand.

"Considering some of the places we've been to, having armor isn't a bad idea."

"Maybe, but I can't exactly carry it around all the time."

"No, but you can teleport it to you, or have Leglin fetch it. In fact, he needs some too."

I put my mug down. "That sounds really expensive."

"Several years back, one of his children wandered off. I found her, and he gave me a lifetime discount." He took a drink of his coffee, watching me.

Even with a discount, custom made armor had to be super expensive. Too expensive for a gift, especially after the practice arena offer I'd already accepted. It wasn't as though we'd progressed to living together, or were planning a wedding. "I don't know."

"Okay, but please think about it. I'd like to keep the promise I made, but it's your decision." His grin was gone, but he didn't look mad.

"I will." Time to change the subject. "I saw something while touching Jeharin's weapons. His memories of seeing you and me together in the Unseelie realm."

"Is that odd?"

"I think so, yeah. He was paying a lot of attention to us, if those memories ended up stored in his weapons."

"Maybe," Logan put his mug down, and reached out to take my hand. "He thought you were gorgeous, and couldn't keep his eyes off you."

I laughed. "Yeah, right. You've seen the elf ladies. They are the definition of gorgeous."

"Not to me." He gave a little tug, and I stepped closer. Both of his hands went to my hips. "But you are."

"Ooh, tell me more." I slid my hands up his chest and over his shoulders.

"Is it too early to cash in that rain check?" He made a face. "Never mind, forget I asked. Seeing dead..."

"Shh." I went to my tiptoes to kiss him. "Let's pretend that part of the night didn't happen."

"I can do that." Logan lowered his head, chasing mine as I dropped back to stand flat-footed. Our lips met and parted, tongues starting a slow dance. I buried one hand in the back of his hair, reveling in the mix of hot coffee and him.

His taste was familiar, a swirl of pine, something nutty, and a slight sweetness. I had yet to remember where I'd tasted it, before we'd ever shared a kiss.

A thump on the back door made me pull back. "What was that?"

"I let the dogs out." Logan sighed. "Guess they're ready to come in."

"Oh." Damn it, I was getting tired of being interrupted. "Well, let's get them in and put to bed."

I was panting and shaking, aftershocks of hot pleasure rippling through my body. "Oh, my God."

Logan kissed his way up until he was on all fours above me, his hands planted on either side of my shoulders. "Does that translate to an A for my efforts?"

"A-plus and two gold stars." Now, I was beginning to feel like jelly inside, all soft and jiggly. I'd hit the freaking jackpot, because the man was an oral wizard. One who'd informed me that "his queen's" pleasure would *always* come first.

"May I advance to the next level?"

"Yes, please." I managed to move, sliding my hands around his sides. He came down lips first, adjusting backward, and I shivered at the feel of his skin slipping along mine. He paused, his forehead against mine, our noses touching. That wasn't the only part of him resting against me.

"I don't want to ruin the mood, but are you sure about the no condom thing?"

"Yes." I moved one hand.

"Okay, just wanted to, oh hey there." Logan lifted his head, his eyes a touch wider as my hand curled around his erection. "Make sure that you were sure, and obviously, you are."

"Definitely." I made a few minor adjustments to our positions. His eyes slowly began to change colors, a smile spreading across his face.

I let go, and he lowered his head, brushing his lips across mine as he pushed inside me. A soft growl escaped him, and my breath caught as his eyes fully lightened. Logan nibbled at my lips, beginning to move, growl trailing off and becoming a low purr. The sound vibrated his chest, causing his chest hair to tickle my breasts, and I laughed.

His lips curved, and he moved to press our cheeks together, allowing him to whisper in my ear. "I love your laugh."

Good, he didn't think I'd laughed at him. Hugging him, I closed my eyes to listen to his purr and the blood rushing in my ears. My awareness of the world beyond the bed receded with each gentle kiss and slow thrust. No rush; he was taking his sweet time and I was totally okay with that.

Nothing to think about but the feel of him in and on me, and the way our bodies moved together. Logan wasn't talking anymore, his lips moving from mine, to my neck, my shoulder, and then back again. We had our own little world, and it was a place I wanted to visit as often as possible.

Everything was slow and sweet and hot for I didn't know how long, but eventually, he began to move faster, his purr deepening, and stopped kissing to press his cheek to mine. He came, a tidal wave of ecstasy pouring out of him to slam into the walls of my mental maze, and spill over their tops.

I wasn't prepared for that, or the results: my body tripping gleefully into another orgasm. "Oh!"

"Mm." Logan stilled, his face buried in my hair and the pillow. I blinked at the ceiling, my hands flat across his back, and wondered *Did that just happen?*

"Mmhm." He relaxed fully for a few seconds, resting his weight on me, and then suddenly raised up to look at me. "You didn't say that, did you?"

"Nope." I was beginning to freak out a smidge. "Um..."

"Do you want me to move?"

I locked my arms around him in answer, still trying to process. "Cordi?"

Focusing on his eyes, I said, "Yes?"

"Calm down." Logan kissed me. "Everything's okay."

He was partially right. It wasn't as though I were in danger. On the other hand, I'd just... psychically vampired him. Fed off his pleasure. That was what happened. Wasn't it? "I didn't do that on purpose."

"You know, having an orgasm isn't the end of the world."

I wanted to laugh, because he was trying to lighten the mood, but couldn't. "But I wasn't going to then you did, and I did, and..." I stopped, catching my breath, aware of another, smaller issue. "I don't really understand what just happened. Also, I didn't realize that um..."

Logan chuckled. "Yes, it's a little messier sans condom. Let's take care of that, and after, we can snuggle and talk. Okay?"

"Okay." I lifted my head to kiss him, feeling guilty as hell.

"I guess it was a heat of the moment slip up?"

"Probably, and that's okay as far as I'm concerned." Logan stroked my arm and kissed the top of my head. "What's important is you being okay with it."

"What if it happens again?"

"Then it does."

"But," I levered myself up to look at him. "It's like, I don't know, cheating or something."

He shook his head. "How about we look at it as sharing? There's no need for you to shoulder blame here."

"But I'm the psychic." I sat completely up, intending to cross my arms, and ended up hugging myself. He moved, sitting up so he could see my face. I felt my eyes begin to water. "I'm ruining it, aren't I?"

"No, sweetheart." He didn't tell me not to cry, but brushed away the tear that fell. "I understand, or think I do, why you're upset. You feel like you did something wrong, violated me in some fashion. Right?"

Shame had me dropping my eyes from his. "I feel like I stole something extremely personal from you."

"No. We care about each a lot, and were having an intimate moment together. Maybe it was just us unconsciously connecting because we were so focused on each other."

Could he be right? I chewed on my bottom lip before looking up. "Do you really think so?"

"I think it's entirely possible. I know I don't want the idea that it might happen again to inhibit you in the future, or worse, scare you away." He stroked my cheek with his fingertips. "We've just started."

"I know." Damn it, I'd completely ruined our first time. "I'm sorry."

Logan froze, his eyes glued to mine, and his fingertips resting on my jaw. "Why?"

"Because I'm freaking out about it."

He relaxed, blowing out a deep breath. "Oh. I thought you were going to leave."

"Not unless you decide I'm too high maintenance."

"I won't. I do think we should agree what happened wasn't bad or wrong though. We're supposed to make each other feel good when making love. You being more empathic than most is a bonus, don't you think?" He smiled, but uncertainly and anxiety radiated from him.

I realized that I was on the verge of blowing us apart, and did my best to calm down. Looking into his eyes, the last thing I wanted to happen was losing him. We *had* just started, and I'd never, ever find another man like him. There couldn't be anyone even close. If what happened didn't bother him, then I shouldn't let it use me for a chew toy. "Right."

Relief caused him to sag. "Still think I love you."

My heart began to thump harder, and I caught his hand to press it to my cheek. "I don't think anymore. I know."

Logan's face lit up as though I'd just saved Christmas from the Grinch.

EIGHTEEN

Something tickled my ear, and I opened my eyes. Logan lay on his side, facing me, one hand tucked under his pillow, the other flat on the bed between us. Our knees were touching, and I smiled, realizing we were mirroring each other.

Busy drinking in his peaceful, sleeping face, I didn't immediately twig to the fact that his bed wasn't in his bedroom any longer. It took another tickle to my ear. I tilted my head back and froze, staring at the large, fluffy, neon purple and teal moth sitting on my pillow.

More moths fluttered above us, in a canopy of leafy green vines. I closed my eyes, re-opened them, and sighed. Canopy and unearthly colored moths were still present. "Seriously?"

"You don't like the bower I made for you?"

I raised my head enough to look over Logan's shoulder. Sal sat on a stone bench a few feet from the bed's edge. He grinned. I didn't.

"Young lovers are such a beautiful sight."

"Wrinkly faced old gods are such creepy perverts." I shooed the moth away, and, keeping hold of the sheet, rose to sit tailor-style, clutching it one-handed to hide my breasts. "Where have you been, and why are you creeping on us?"

"It's true some time has passed since we last spoke. You were perturbed, if you'll remember, and I thought I should give you some space." A pale pink and dark turquoise moth landed on his shoulder. Sal reached up to stroke its furry thorax.

I gave Logan a gentle poke in the stomach. He didn't react. "Why is he still asleep?"

"This is a private conversation. Now tell me, how has my favorite psychic been?"

Past experience said the little god wouldn't go away until he was satisfied. "Fine. I mean, aside from learning that demons had some of my blood and hair, had hexed me with delusions, oh, and were again planning to slit me from stem to stern."

Sal bobbed his head. "Yes, I completely forgot to mention that. I meant to, but handling the Unseelie/Morpheus situation seemed more important at the time."

Prick. "Thanks a lot. You could've saved me a little grief there."

"You apparently sorted it out just fine. Go on." His wrinkles rearranged into an expression of expectancy.

"Well, let's see." I adjusted the sheet over Logan, making sure his butt was covered. "Maeve wants me to marry Thorandryll, and he's not exactly against the plan."

Sal waved that away. "I'm sure you can handle it. How's your family? Your delightful mother, and those two cute little brothers?"

I cocked my head, my eyes narrowing. "Why do you want to know?"

He laughed. "So suspicious. You care for them, I care about you. Therefore, I care about them too."

Uh huh. I needed to keep a closer eye on my little brothers. Wasn't there a chance one or both of them might turn out to be psychic? We shared a father. "They're fine."

"Hm, and what about this?" He gestured at Logan.

"None of your damn business."

Sal chortled, dropping his hand. "Oh, having your tiger trapped is new."

"He's not trapped." What would happen if I tried to smack his smug, wrinkled face? Probably nothing good.

"Oh, but he is, and willingly so. He's a fine young man, your Logan. It's good to see how much your judgment has improved."

Did I care about his approval? No. No, I did not. "How about you do me a favor and pay Maeve a little visit? Give her something besides me to think about?"

The little god shook his head. "I'm afraid that's your situation to take care of."

"Really, what good is it doing me to have you for a fairy godfather?" I tugged the sheet higher and switched hands. "You drop in, tell me I'm doing it wrong or that you can't help with stuff, and then you're out. As a bonus, when you need a ride, you don't bother asking before jumping in."

Sal petted the moth again. "You're still perturbed about that, I see."

Actually, I was getting angry about it. I hadn't at the time, with everything else going on, but now? Oh, yeah. I was hot. "Wouldn't you be pissed, if someone did that to you?"

He sobered, and met my eyes. "I sincerely apologize for our trespass, Discordia. It was necessary that you weren't aware of our presence, or things may have gone quite a bit differently."

Sal's sincerity calmed me down a touch. "Why was it necessary?"

"If you'd been aware of being our vessel, others would've discovered us, and we likely wouldn't have made it to the cavern where Morpheus was imprisoned." He lowered his chin. "We gods are not united, child. Some of us work to maintain the world's balance, while others crave chaos and destruction."

I shuddered, and wished Logan would wake up. I needed a hug. "Sal, I really, truly don't want to be involved in whatever you gods have going on."

"It's not a matter of 'want.' The choices you've made in the past have already placed you on my side. You chose to use your power to become a crusader. You make daily decisions to right wrongs and help others. You," Sal stabbed his forefinger in my direction. "Are the one who chooses your path."

Apparently, wanting to be good and useful had screwed me when it came to the god stuff. I felt a pout forming, and forced myself to stop it. He dropped his hand again, and looked at Logan. "Do you love your young man?"

I bristled, ready to launch myself over Logan and attack Sal to protect him. "Yes, and don't you dare..."

"Oh, shut up. I'm not going to threaten him. He's good for you, and if he's also part of your happiness, then that's all the better." A grin rearranged his wrinkles again. "Cernunnos even has a bit of approval for him, and let me say, getting that one to approve of a shifter is practically impossible."

I wanted to know, so asked. "Why?"

"Because he's the Horned God, Lord of the Hunt, and Level One Billion Master of Animals. Shifters are no longer mere animals. They were taken from him. He's not a god who forgives lesser beings for taking away his toys."

"Oh." It suddenly made sense, Logan's not being affected by the Hunt until he'd changed shapes. And Cernunnos' sharp "You, a tiger who walks in the shape of a man?" before he'd delegated Logan to the role of being my servant.

It seemed that since I'd vowed to do better, I was learning useful things at a faster rate. Go figure.

"Well, my time's up for now. Gotta run." Sal shooed the moth from his shoulder and stood.

"Wait. We're on a case, and..."

"Yes. Word of advice: What appears obvious isn't always the truth." He stared at me. "You need to walk with extreme care, Discordia. Don't depend on just your powers."

"Does that mean another god's involved in the case?"

He smiled. "It means you shouldn't forget you have more than one option, when it comes to protecting yourself. Or," he nodded at Logan. "Those you love. Surprise people. Good chat, see you later."

And boom, he was gone. I twisted and dropped down on my back, scowling up at the rainbow of moths and greenery. I hadn't had the chance to ask him about Petra's theory. "It sucks, being his favorite psychic."

A fat, furry blue moth with yellow legs and antennae landed on my face. Dust fell from its wings. I sneezed...

"Whoa." I opened my eyes, catching Logan in the act of pulling back the cup of coffee he'd been holding close to my nose.

Which was running a little. Gross. I sniffled. "Sorry."

"Let me get you a tissue, and a fresh cup." He put the cup on the nightstand. I sat up and threw off the covers.

"I'll get it. Have to use the bathroom anyway. Oh." I was naked. So was he. "We can't start your cooking lessons nude. Something important could get burned."

Logan smiled. "I was hoping we could hold off for an hour or so before starting them."

I returned his smile while leaving the bed. "Hold that thought until I get back."

Two hours later, we were finally dressed and in the kitchen. I felt fantastic, relieved we hadn't had a repeat of the inadvertent mental linkage when his moment arrived. "The biggest trick is selecting the right temperature to cook with. Get in a hurry and turn up the heat too much, and you'll be scorching or burning food left and right."

"I'll remember that." Logan poured the whipped eggs into the waiting skillet. "So he knew about the hex and forgot to tell you?"

"That's what he said." I'd told him about Sal's visit, during our after cuddles, but had skipped the parts where we'd talked about him. "You don't have to stir them constantly, but don't let them sit too long either."

"Okay." He traded me the bowl for the spatula I was holding. "How do I know when it's time to stir?"

"Watch the edges." I went to the sink and rinsed out the bowl, not caring how domestic we were being. "Give the eggs a good stir when the edges start looking a little dry."

"Right." Intent on the skillet, he said, "Sounds like the Morpheus thing would've gone sideways if he'd asked pretty please."

"Sal made it sound that way." I looked out the window over the sink, checking on the dogs. They were playing. Logan's backyard didn't have a fence, but a line of tall shrubbery marked its dimensions. The sun was shining, and it wasn't too cold to hike to the meadow. I wondered what the weather was like outside the territory.

Returning to the stove, I hugged Logan from behind and peeked over his shoulder at the skillet. "Doing good. I have a question."

"Which is?"

"Can you get your pocket realm to pass you secret messages?"

Logan stirred the eggs. "Our pocket realm. Yes, and it's necessary, to keep everything maintained properly."

"You heard me asking Thorandryll about ward alarms, right?"

"I did. Yes, he probably does have his realm letting him know when you show up unannounced." He patted my clasped hands. "If I'd known you were wondering, I would've told you once I learned about that."

"No problem. I wasn't actually curious about it until last night. But I have been dying to know how he always has the right number of chairs for guests, even when he didn't know I was coming, or who with."

Logan laughed. "Remind me, you need to be hooked into our realm. It recognizes you, but it's not going to respond much until you're bonded to it."

My forearms and hands were getting too warm, being close to the skillet. I gave him a final squeeze and moved to the side. "Gonna guess that blood's required?"

"Yes, just a few drops." He was not looking away from the skillet, and his seriousness was quickly becoming amusing. "If anything ever happens, and we're invaded here, we all need to be bound to the realm. It'll help, change to confuse the enemy, and other things."

"Wow. That sounds, I don't even know." I frowned. "So it's alive?"

"Not exactly. It's more like," he paused to stir the eggs again. They were almost done. "Like artificial intelligence. But magic artificial intelligence."

"Go ahead and add the cheese." I pushed the bag of shredded cheddar closer to him. Logan quickly sprinkled a healthy handful over the eggs. "Let it melt, give the eggs a good final chopping stir, and they're done."

"Okay." Someone knocked on the front door, and he looked at me. "Can you get that?"

"Yep." I left the kitchen, smiling, but also hoping he didn't let the cheese melt too long. Reaching the front door, I opened it wide. "Hey."

Terra's scowl become a big smile. "Hi. What are you doing... oh. Ooh."

Laughing, I pulled her inside and into a hug. "Logan's cooking breakfast. Come on in."

"You do know he's worse at cooking than I am, right?" She flipped her pale braid over her shoulder. "I mean, than I was. I'm better now, thanks to you."

"He decided he needed cooking lessons too." We walked back to the kitchen, to find Logan moving the skillet to a hot pad while turning off the stove. "Okay, let me see the results."

He'd gone stiff, and moving back to let me check the eggs, half-bowed to Terra. "My Queen."

"Stop it!" She was suddenly in tears. I tried to make myself as small as possible as the tension in the room ratcheted up twenty notches. "Stop being so, so..."

Logan went to her, pulling her into a hug. Terra sobbed on his shoulder. "I hate fighting with you."

"I don't like fighting with you either." He stroked her hair, beginning to rock slightly. "I love you, and just want what's best for you. I want you to be happy."

"I am," she wailed, her hands clenching into fists against his back. "Except for us fighting over it."

He didn't say anything for a few seconds, and spoke slowly when he did. "If you're truly happy, then I'm okay with it."

Terra pulled back, her hands relaxing, to look up. Her face was pink and tear-stained. "Really?"

"Yes." He pulled her back against his chest and kissed the top of her head. "Really."

I tiptoed across the kitchen and slipped out the back door to give them a few minutes alone.

NINETEEN

We'd forgotten our morning engagement with David, and were on our way to the Blue Orb to make up for it. Logan slowed the car for a turn. "Sorry breakfast was cold."

"It warmed up nicely. Microwaves are useful things. Besides, I'm just glad you and Terra are good again."

"I'm sorry, it sounds like Logan cooked breakfast." Dane leaned forward to look at him. "Did you cook breakfast?"

"Under her expert eye."

"And neither of you thought to invite me?"

I kissed his cheek. "Sorry. It was a private breakfast."

"Why was," he paused, sniffing at me. Turning his head, he sniffed at Logan. "Oh."

As my face began warming, Logan elbowed him in the chest. "Do you remember that talk we had about behaving like humans in public?"

"Yes." Dane eased all the way into the back seat, out of his reach. "But Cordi's clan."

I was currently a rather red-faced clan member. Logan patted my thigh, and shot Dane a Look via the rearview mirror. "We do not sniff at each other in public."

"Sorry, Cordi. I won't sniff you again."

"I'd appreciate that. Um, does that mean we smell like..." Sex, I was going to ask, but Logan answered before I finished.

"Our scents are mingled. That's what he smelled."

"Oh." We'd taken a shower together before cooking breakfast. Good to know we didn't smell like stale sex, because eww. "I guess that means everyone with a good nose can smell us on each other?"

"Yes." Logan glanced at me. "It happens with everyone. We're simply able to smell it."

I remembered Nick smelling Thorandryll on me, the day the elf had macked on me. "I knew that, just didn't occur to me right then."

"It's stronger when two people have..."

"Dane," Logan warned.

"I'm not going to tease. When two people have been intimate, their scents mingle more."

"I see." Basically, every shifter we were around was going to know we'd had sex. I was not exactly cool with that idea. No one needed to know what was going on in my personal life, unless I chose to share it with them.

On the other hand, I kind of liked the idea that Thorandryll might pick up on it, at our four o'clock meeting. "How good are elf noses?"

Dane laughed. Logan grinned, guiding the car around another, slower vehicle. "Not as good as ours, but better than humans'."

"Does the uh, scent mingling get stronger, the more often we're intimate?"

"Yes."

"Is that what you meant about marking territory?"

A choking gurgle came from the back seat, and Logan flushed, but gamely replied. "Yes."

I grinned. "I thought you wanted me to bite you."

More gurgles, and the sound of a fist pounding the back seat. Logan's flush grew darker. He was practically tomato red now. Which is why I wasn't expecting him to say, "Oh, you can bite me."

I began laughing. Dane seemed to be having a fit of some sort, and I twisted around to take a look at him. He had his head back, face bright pink and contorted. Tears slipped from the corners of his eyes, his teeth were clenched tight, and he was pounding on the seat with one fist. His chest was heaving. "You okay?"

That apparently did it for him. Roars of laughter poured forth, and before I knew it, Logan and I were laughing with him. I don't know how we didn't end up in a wreck, but we made it safely to the shop.

⚜

"Ow, I hurt now." I wiped my eyes, my cheeks aching. I had to rub them next. "Do I look like a raccoon?"

"No." Logan's eyelashes were damp. "Little smear under your right eye."

I flipped the sun visor down to use the mirror. "I don't even know what was so funny to you, Dane."

"All of it." He sighed. "I needed that. A good laugh clears the head."

Logan moved in his seat until he could see Dane. "Trouble?"

"Nothing major. Sheila and I had a difference of opinion last night. A political one. She thinks Thorandryll as mayor would be awesome."

"Why?" I flipped the visor back into place.

"Because he's an elf and must be smarter, and wiser, than any human candidate. She also mentioned that she and all her friends think he's hot." Dane frowned. "I don't talk about how hot other women are when we're on a date."

Ouch. I couldn't think of anything to say to him. Logan could. "Stop seeing her."

We both stared at him. He glanced at me, but met Dane's eyes. "I'm serious. You can be overly exuberant at times, but you're respectful to women. Doesn't sound like she's returning the favor."

"But I like her."

"Then tell her how it made you feel. How she responds will tell you all you need to know." Logan moved to face front again, and opened his door. He got out, and I followed suit, pulling my seat forward for Dane to exit.

Little harsh on the advice side, I 'pathed to Logan.

He met my eyes over the top of the car. *You didn't meet his last girlfriend. I'd fill you in, but that's his story to share, if he ever wants to.*

And I'm not a shifter.

Logan's lips parted, and he shook his head once. *I didn't mean...*

No, I was reminding myself. That I needed to have a good sit-down with him, and walk away with a better understanding of what it meant to be clan.

We went into the shop, which wasn't busy. Tonya was in one of the aisles with a customer, because I could hear her answering a question. Jo and David were behind the counter, unpacking stock. "Six red-pillar style."

"Hm... yep, got them." She saw us, and tapped him on the head with her pen. "They're here."

David straightened. "Hello, ow." He rubbed his lower back. "I'll go get the charm."

"Thanks. Sorry we're running so late."

Trixie, Jo's familiar, leaped onto the counter. "Mrow."

"Hello to you too." I stroked the cat's back. She sauntered a few steps, halting to look up at Logan. He scratched under her chin. As Trixie moved on to Dane, I grinned at Jo. "What's shakin', bacon?"

"Ha. Not much." She lowered her voice, shooting a glance in the direction of Tonya's voice while leaning toward me. "Tonya's going to try for a familiar Saturday night. Do you think you could make it?"

"What time?"

"Eleven-thirty. PM, not AM. She'll need to prepare and be ready by midnight."

"I'll be here if I can. It's a big step, right?"

A proud smile lit up Jo's face. "Yes, but we're sure she's ready for it. She's a quick learner, and more importantly, level-headed. It's time she moves to the next level."

"Yay. Do I need to bring anything?"

"Yourself, and positive thoughts." Jo straightened, using her fingers to whisk her auburn bangs out of her eyes. "Shh, here she comes."

I leaned back to look past the guys, and saw the teen witch walking down the back aisle, Nate Brock behind her.

He saw me and smiled. "Well, well, well. If it isn't Miss Jones."

Crap. I traded a look with Logan, and Jo asked, "Do you know him?"

"He's the reporter."

Her hazel eyes rounded. David came out of the back room, charm in hand. "You'll have to go outside for Logan and Dane to test whether or not they can smell its magic."

Jo spun, dragging a forefinger across her throat with a hiss to get his attention. David blinked at her, nose scrunching as he pushed up his glasses. "What?"

"Reporter."

"Where?" His mild blue eyes traveled to a frozen Tonya and the still-smiling Brock. "Oh, dear."

"So, your name's Dane. That would be Dane Soames, who works for Arcane Solutions?"

Damn, he was really good.

"It's a private investigation agency owned by a Mr. Whitehaven. But you know that, don't you, Mr. Soames?" Brock chuckled when Dane ignored him. "Not ringing any bells? Funny, Miss Sheila Taylor was positive her boyfriend's last name was Soames."

David lurched forward, blinking furiously. "Very sorry, we're closing for lunch. That means you'll have to leave."

"Miss Jones sure has a lot of people willing to protect her. Why is that?" The reporter stepped around Tonya, walking to the end of the counter. "A lot of supes willing to, I should say."

Trixie arched her back, hissing at him. He ignored her. "You people. What is it with you?"

"Lunch. Closing. Leave," David said, his tone unyielding. He even pointed at the door.

"Or what, Mr. Thornby? Will you cast a spell? Throw a curse?" Brock folded his arms and rested them on the counter. "See, unless one of you feels like dealing with an assault charge, there's not much you can do to make me go away."

As David slowly lowered his arm, the reporter focused on me. "Except you, Miss Jones. Answer my questions, and your friends and family won't ever hear another peep from me."

Yeah, right. But maybe he'd follow us out, and leave them alone for now. I reached out, and David deposited the charm into my hand. "Thanks."

"No problem."

Behind us, the door opened. Jo's sharp intake of air closed my eyes. What now?

Kethyrdryll's "Lady Discord" rang out. Well, crap, there was the cherry on top. Opening my eyes, I turned around.

"Prince Thorandryll." Brock straightened to make a beeline for the elf. Kethyrdryll wasn't alone. Edrel and Midnight—I should probably make an attempt to find out the dude's name—were with him, both reaching for their swords.

"Nate Brock, your Highness. I'm with the *Santo Trueno Daily.* May I ask you a few..."

"You've mistaken me for my brother." Kethyrdryll's pleased smile had been replaced with an arrogant mask that would've done his brother proud. "I do not speak with reporters."

Brock ignored the last part. "Can you confirm your brother and Miss Jones' relationship, Lord Kethyrdryll?"

I smiled as the elf simply stared at the man, even though his silence didn't deter the reporter. "Is it true there's wedding bells in the future for the happy couple?"

Oh, now, that was going way too far. I had to bite my tongue to keep from speaking.

Edrel frowned, his brow wrinkling, and shook his head. A blink later, and he was in front of Brock, his sword's point an inch from the reporter's neck. "You will cease your attempt to see my thoughts now."

"I'll see you in prison if you touch me." Brock looked a little pale.

"Maybe you'll be cell mates," I said, and smiled as everyone looked at me. "You assaulted him first, trying to break into his mind. In fact, you've also assaulted me. Maybe Edrel and I should see about filing charges."

"With what proof?"

I tapped my temple. "I'm sure the police can arrange for a psychic to collect our memories of your assaults."

Copernicus fluttered down from somewhere to land on Edrel's shoulder. The raven settled his wings, focusing a beady eye on the reporter. His rusty croaking made Brock flinch. "Amateur. Humans don't feel your digging. All others do."

For the first time since we'd met, Brock opened his mouth and no words came out. He closed it, and without further ado, carefully edged around the elves and left the shop.

Jo huffed. "Well, that was fun."

"I didn't know it was him." Tonya had finally thawed.

"It's okay. He's gone now, and I bet he won't be back. Copernicus scared him off." And unfortunately, had confirmed I was one of those "others," but the reporter likely already knew that. Why else would he be so interested?

"I'm pleased to meet you." Kethyrdryll, wearing a bright smile, shook David's hand. "Lady Discord has spoken highly of you."

"She has?"

"Of course, I have." I gave David's shoulder a light smack. "And I have the feeling you two are going to become good friends."

David raised his eyebrows. "Me and an elf?"

"He's met my brother, hasn't he?"

I laughed. "Yes, he has. David, he's nothing like Thorandryll or Alleryn. Why don't you tell him about your demon time theory?"

That was all it took. They were in deep conversation before I took two steps away. Logan and Dane were waiting for me by the door. Smiling, I said, "I knew they'd take a shine to each other."

"We may never see them again. They're headed into the back." Dane pulled the door open.

I stepped out first, checking the cul de sac for any sign of Brock, or the sedan we'd seen him in at the museum. "Ahh. Maybe he'll decide I'm not worth the trouble."

"Wouldn't get my hopes up." Logan caught my hand. "He's a predator."

"I refuse to be his prey. How far from the shop do we need to go?"

"Let's walk to the end of the block."

We did, and Dane spoke for them both. "We can smell the magic from the charm."

"Okay, my curiosity is satisfied." I dropped the charm into my coat pocket. "So they must be using the unwashed clothing trick. My question is: Where are they getting it from?"

"Can we speculate over lunch? And someone better call the boss." Dane's jaw clenched, and he looked down. "I need to make a call, too."

Logan squeezed his shoulder, and his voice was gentle when he said, "We'll wait by the car."

"Thanks." The younger man pulled out his phone as we walked away.

"Does he have to break things off over that?"

"She proved unworthy of his trust." Logan put his arm around my waist. "He asked if he should warn her about talking to reporters, so I know he did."

"Oh." I glanced back. Dane's eyes were closed, his shoulders sagging, as he spoke into his phone. "I feel bad for him."

TWENTY

"Let's start with 'what do we know.'" I dipped a chip into the bowl of salsa. "Dane?"

"Logan's the new guy on the team."

"Officially, I am. But," Logan held up a finger. "Unofficially, I began helping with cases before you did."

"Okay." Dane slouched back and sighed. "We know that someone is stealing magical artifacts and killing people. We know the killers have psychic abilities, and they're fast."

"We know that all three stolen objects won't work without the proper code words," I added. "Tanisha said the stick didn't work, and the boots needed a code word. Thorandryll said his stolen ring requires a code word, too."

"That's all we know as fact." Logan moved the chip basket closer to Dane's side of the table. The younger shifter was in a deep funk. "We think they're vampires, because of the precise use of psychic abilities. Also because it doesn't seem necessary for them to kill, but they do, and because the crimes have occurred after sunset."

"That's all we have." Dane ignored the chips. "Except we also think they're masking their scent by wearing humans' unwashed clothing."

I ate another chip. "That's kind of a sticking point for me. Where do they get pre-worn clothing?"

"Blood donors?" Logan selected a chip, nudging the basket another half inch in Dane's direction.

"But does that make sense? I mean, they've killed people during break-ins. Do you really think they have donors instead of more victims?"

"Good point." Dane finally noticed the chips and salsa. He straightened. "They're killing for kicks, not to feed, during the break-ins."

My phone went off, and I checked the display. "Derrick or Stone. I need to pick a ringtone for them." I answered. "Jones here."

"Hello." It was Derrick. "I'm afraid I have both good and bad news to report."

"Bad first, please."

"We've accounted for and confirmed alibis for our people who have pyrokinesis or teleportation."

Well, so much for the killers being from the Barrows. "What's the good news?"

He chuckled. "It's not any of our people."

I made a face. "Funny. But yeah, good news. Have..."

"I've already informed Detective Herde, and offered my help during the dark hours, should he need the assistance of a master vampire."

"That's awesome of you. I have news too." I told him about Brock's visit to the Blue Orb. "I think he'll be more careful around supes in the future."

"I would think so. Yet, now he has..."

"Yeah, if he's realized it." I paused, looking at Dane. "Does Sheila know what I am?"

He winced. "She knows your name and that you're a PI. We introduced ourselves to her, remember?"

"Right, sorry." I spotted our waitress headed to our table. "Okay, our lunch is being served. I guess we'll see you tonight."

"Of course. Farewell."

"Bye." I waited until our plates were down and the waitress had left before asking, "Anyone need that repeated?"

"No bad little vamps in the Barrows." Dane's smile lacked its usual joy, but he dug into his enchiladas with a healthy appetite.

Damian didn't need us, even though the killers had struck again the previous night, at a private residence. I had a couple hours before my meeting with Thorandryll. We returned to clan territory. Leaving Dane to the tender mercies of my Tinies, and the sisterly care of Alanna, we set off for the meadow with the big dogs in tow.

"He's pretty down."

Logan sighed. "It always hits him hard when things don't work out."

"But he'll be okay, right?" Heartbreak sucked ass.

"Sure. It'll take him a while, but Dane has an optimistic soul. All we have to do is keep him from brooding too much for a couple weeks." Logan stepped onto a fallen log and offered me his hand. "In two or three months, he'll be noticing other women exist again."

He knew Dane better than I did, having lived with him for years. I nodded. "Subject change then. I don't fully understand what it means to be clan."

"It's the same as being family, except with people who've mutually selected each other. No one goes without; we all work together to keep the coffers filled, and everyone safe." Logan kept hold of my hand as we hopped off the log. "Terra's making some changes now that we have this place."

"Oh?" I took a deep breath, loving the smell of crisp, piney air.

"Good changes. She decided to end full tithing. We have more members now, and we're a hell of a lot better off than we were."

Bone leaped out of the undergrowth, stood on his hind legs and took a few steps. "Rrrrr, I'm a bear."

"I'm pretty sure you're a goofball, not a bear." He dropped to all fours and ran off ahead. "What's the new tithe?"

"Fifty percent."

I wrinkled my nose. "That still seems pretty high."

Logan began swinging our joined hands. "It's fair. Practically everything's provided, aside from food, clothing, and gas. Actually, for those with lower paying jobs, we have clothing, and canned and dry food in the store rooms in the main building."

Ah. No matter what, everyone was taken care of. "I see. Will that be a draw for new recruits?"

"We're hoping so. Meadow's just ahead."

I had to ask. "Exactly how do I fit in?"

"This," he swung his free arm wide, "wouldn't be ours, if not for you. You're exempt from tithing for life. Anything you need, just ask. If we can do it, we will."

"Not really comfortable with the idea." I wasn't. It just didn't feel right to even think about asking friends for financial help, or anything beyond what they already did for me. Assuming I ever needed financial help, or whatever.

"Cordi, we can't put a price on having our own pocket realm, knowing that we're safe, and have everything we need. And in far shorter time than we'd hoped." Logan pulled me to a halt and turned to face me. "You did that. Saved us years of work."

"Damn, I'm good."

He laughed and kissed me. "You are. If you need something, just ask. You're clan, you have the right to ask."

"Okay." I had no intention of asking for anything big, ever. Doggy daycare and a practice arena was more than enough.

"I'm serious. Doesn't matter what." He kissed me again, on the forehead. "Come on, let's go see your meadow."

He was turning when Diablo tore free of the underbrush and rushed across our path. There was a small, orange splotch on his back. "Get it off! Get it off!"

The black pit disappeared into the trees. I looked at Logan. "I'm sorry, was that a monkey riding my dog?"

"It was. A baby tamarin. We need to get it back to the right area." Logan frowned. "Diablo won't eat it, will he?"

"Diablo!" I let go of Logan's hand to pursue my dog.

It was five after four when I teleported to Thorandryll's front door. Catching a panicked pit bull with a screeching, baby monkey on his back hadn't been the easiest thing in the world. A pine needle fell out of my hair while I was reaching for the door knocker. "Lovely."

There hadn't been time to clean up. I ran my fingers through my hair. More needles, and ouch, a couple of twigs, came loose. Edrel opened the door. "Lady Di... ah."

"Hi there." I dropped my hands, plastering a huge smile on my face. "Sorry I'm late. There was a problem."

"I see." He stepped back. "Do come in."

"Do you ever get a day off?" I walked in, well aware of the messy trail I was leaving. Heavy treads could collect a lot of dirt.

"Of course. Would you care to freshen up before I escort you to the prince?"

"No, I'm already late. Better go on in." Was there dirt on my face? Probably. I'd face-planted three separate times, the third thanks to Bone. I was pretty sure he'd done it on purpose, too.

"As you wish." Edrel's lips were twitching.

"You can laugh. I won't be offended."

He took me at my word, and proved to have a nice laugh, low and friendly sounding. Edrel didn't overdo it either, but he was still smiling when we reached Thorandryll's study. "Your Highness, my lord, Lady Discord has arrived."

I walked in, and instantly wished I'd taken my guide's offer to take the time to freshen up. Lady Celadine's sneer was a scorcher, as she gave me a raking once over before turning to Thorandryll. "She's not fit to be in our presence."

Okay, it appeared I was wrong about the reason for the meeting. "Sorry I'm late."

Kethyrdryll, standing behind the desk and to one side, smiled. "It appears there was situation."

I headed for the empty chair beside Celadine's. Too late to go clean up now. "A baby monkey mistook one of my dogs for its mommy. My dog wasn't thrilled."

Thorandryll, elbow planted on his desk, dropped his forehead into his hand. Face hidden, his shoulders began quivering. I was just amusing the hell out of everyone.

"You smell." Celadine leaned away from me, her nose wrinkled.

"Yeah, like dirt and trees. You're an elf. Deal with it." I slouched back in my chair, stretched out my legs, and crossed my ankles.

Thorandryll cleared his throat while lifting his head. His eyes were bright, and he wasn't quite pulling off the sternness he was trying for. "Lady Celadine has made a breach of contract complaint."

"We found and returned her stolen mirror. It's on display at the museum, just like it was supposed to be."

She rounded on me. "Don't pretend ignorance, girl. It was returned without its occupant."

"You hired us to find your stolen mirror. You didn't specify 'spirit still attached,'" I pointed out. Splitting hairs, just to watch the tips of her ears turn red. "I didn't remove the spirit from your mirror. The demons did."

Her glare would've melted steel. "You filthy little guttersnipe."

Thorandryll finally achieved his stern face. "I'll thank you to remember where you are, Celadine."

She lifted her nose, turning to look at him. "What can you possibly see in this, this... she's..."

"Quiet." Celadine zipped her lips, and Thorandryll looked at me. "The spirit was transferred to another mirror, which you also retrieved. Why didn't you turn that mirror over to her?"

"It didn't belong to her." I waited until his eyebrows drew down before saying more. "Actually, the original mirror probably doesn't belong to her either."

Thorandryll's eyebrows returned to normal. "And you determined that how, exactly?"

"I didn't determine anything. The gargoyle queen did. She helped us retrieve the second mirror and something else." I held his stare. I'd been impetuous, acting on Petra saying the mirror spirit belonged to my bloodline the way I had. But I wasn't going to back down. Backing down showed weakness, and I couldn't appear weak. Not to any elves. "Petra said that the mirror and spirit belonged to my bloodline. Mr. Whitehaven said he wasn't going to argue with her. Are you?"

"Gargoyles do not lie," Kethyrdryll murmured.

"If the spirit belongs to my bloodline—by the way, Cernunnos is the one who stuck the poor guy in that mirror, and according to Petra, he's one of the gods I'm descended from—then I'm kind of wondering how she," I flipped my hand at Celadine. "Managed to get her hands on it."

"Through great expense," she snapped.

"Got a receipt? Or was it expensive to hire a burglar?" I smiled at her. She sneered back, the tips of her ears lobster red. "A spirit that's also a grimoire doesn't sound like something that goes on the auction block often."

Thorandryll sighed. "How did you acquire the mirror, Celadine?"

"I paid dearly for it." She didn't meet his eyes.

"Who did you purchase it from?" I shivered, because the prince's voice had turned icy. She mumbled some name. "I'll contact him, and ask where he obtained it."

As he began to reach for his phone, she shot me a look of pure, narrow-eyed and teeth-bared hatred. "He stole it."

Thorandryll put his phone down. "You purchased stolen goods, and dared to trouble me over the rightful owner's heir claiming those goods?"

"Uh oh, somebody's in trouble," I sang under my breath. The prince shot me a dark look. "Sorry."

"I have possessed that mirror for..."

"You can keep the mirror," I said. "I don't want it. The spirit though, maybe his body's gone, but he's still a person. This, in case you didn't catch it, is America. We don't allow slavery here."

"Yet, you kept it."

I shook my head. "Nope."

"Then where is it?" Celadine's knuckles were turning white as she clamped onto her chair's arms.

"He's somewhere safe, where no one will be able to use him." I had an idea. "And he's staying there until I can talk Cernunnos into freeing him."

All three elves simply stared at me. I flicked a pine needle off my jeans. "So, are we done here? I have a party to get ready for."

"Insufferable, smug little bitch." Celadine raised her hand, fingers beginning to move.

"Do not." Thorandryll's glare froze her. "I don't want my study destroyed when Miss Jones retaliates."

I wondered what she'd been about to do. He kept talking. "Unless you care to dispute it, my decision is that Miss Jones retains ownership of the spirit as her family property." He narrowed his eyes. "And I really wouldn't dispute it, Celadine."

She sniffed, rose, and curtsied. "Your Highness. May I take my leave?"

"Please do."

Celadine left, but not without shooting me a final venomous glare. Once she'd cleared the room, I prepared to get up. "If that's all..."

"Please stay seated, Miss Jones."

"Why?"

"We have another matter to discuss."

Oh, joy.

TWENTY-ONE

I settled back into the chair, re-crossed my ankles, and smiled. Thorandryll smiled back. Kethyrdryll clasped his hands together, a faint smile on his lips. No one said anything. I gave it a few seconds before pulling my phone out of my coat pocket to check the time.

"It's four-thirty, and I have somewhere to be at seven. I'm going to need time to take a shower and dress. So, spit it out."

"I'm afraid you made an enemy." Thorandryll gestured at the doorway while sitting back.

"She'll have to get in line behind the demons, thanks to you."

His smile disappeared. "It was never my intention to make you a target."

"Maybe not, but hey!" I did double finger-guns at him and winked. "You did."

"I paid a high price for my error. Do you ever intend to forgive me for it?"

I was in the mood for another Come to Jesus meeting. "I honestly don't know, because that's not the only mistake you've made. You know, before you came along, my life was pretty simple. I found stuff, located missing people, and ashed the occasional vamp. Now, I have to keep a constant watch for demons, reporters, and your mother."

Kethyrdryll's lips were pressed in a tight line, his dark blue eyes slightly wide. Thorandryll's eyebrows had drawn together. "There's been something different about you lately, Miss Jones."

"You're absolutely right. I'm not the same girl I was, and congratulations, you played a part in who I've become." I paused. "I have responsibilities I never thought I would, to my clan and my allies. I have to worry about my family being harmed or used. But I've also learned a lot about who I am, and what I am. I've finally decided to own it."

"I see." The smile on Thorandryll's face made it clear he thought I was just talking. Making noise that didn't really mean anything.

I studied him for a moment before shaking my head. "I don't think you do. I didn't choose any of this, except for my adoption by the clan. But here I am, and you'd better listen up: I will not be manipulated any longer. Not by you, not by your mother, not by anyone."

"I'm not going to be controlled according to what others think is best, or because they're afraid of me or what I may do in the future. What I am going to do is this: I'm going to protect the people I care about. I'm going to keep doing my best to help people. If that's not to your, or anyone else's liking, tough cookies. Newsflash: I'm not your bitch."

Kethyrdryll burst into applause, and I shot him a quick smile. Thorandryll seemed frozen, but recovered and turned his head to glare at his twin. The other clapped a few more times before dropping his hands and managing to suppress his smile.

The prince turned back to me, a frown etching deep lines other either side of his mouth. He suddenly looked far older than thirty. "I'm afraid my focus on the future has caused my missteps with you, Miss Jones. I, too, only wish to protect those I care for, and the innocent." He leaned forward, crossing his arms and resting them on his desk. "I don't believe it's too late for us to come to a working agreement."

"I'm not going to marry you, and unless you start treating all other species with the common courtesy they deserve, I'm not going to be your ally." *There, stick that in your pipe and smoke it, Your Highness.* I crossed my arms and waited for his response.

For once, Thorandryll seemed to be at a complete loss. He was silent for several seconds, his expression neutral as we watched each other. With a single shake of his head, he finally spoke. "Firstly, please accept my sincere apologies for my actions, and the repercussions they've had for you."

Behind him, his brother's eyebrows shot upward. I had to pretend to cough, to cover my mouth before I smiled. Dropping my hand, I picked a few pine needles off my coat. "Are you asking for a clean slate?"

"Yes, I am. Please."

So polite. I looked at him again. "Okay, you're forgiven, but don't expect me to forget."

"Thank you, and I don't." Thorandryll took a deep breath. "This is a new world, and a new time. I've been allowing the past to rule me, when choosing to fully adapt is the wiser choice."

Well, that sounded promising. Enough for me to offer him a smile. "Great."

He straightened, unfolding his arms and sitting back. "We need to show a united front, Miss Jones. Not only for your protection, but for ours—the whole of Santo Trueno's supernatural community. Lord Derrick and I are the faces of that community now, but you'll be joining us soon."

"Not by choice," I pointed out. "I'd still be flying under the media radar, if not for you. And just in case you're thinking it, no, I'm not going to pretend to be your girlfriend."

A half-smile crossed his face. "I'll ban the hunting of shifters."

"Good idea, but you should've already done that." I hadn't heard about any hunts. Then again, I didn't know every shifter group in the city.

"You're correct, I should have. I'll rectify my mistake." Thorandryll gave a nod. "The Council is small, and in need of new blood. We're hidebound, too few of us willing to attempt forcing changes through."

I held up my hand. "I do not want to be on the Council, if that's where you're heading. I have enough on my plate."

"Then would you be open to accompanying me to a meeting, now and then? I think it would be good for you to gain an understanding of the Council and its members."

Ugh, endless meetings with bickering supe politicians? Let me think: Nope, with a side of hell, no. "I'll think about it."

Heh, maybe I was cut out for politics.

Thorandryll nodded. "I'm afraid it won't be an easy process, yet I believe it's time we give seats to the leaders, or elected representatives, of each supernatural species."

I was speechless, because that was A Really Huge Thing. My eyes went from him to Kethyrdryll, who was beaming. He nodded. I found my tongue. "Are you serious?"

"Deadly serious, Miss Jones."

Uncrossing my ankles, I sat up straight. "Can you make that happen?"

Thorandryll nodded. "I swear by Danu it will happen."

He'd sworn by Danu before, and Logan had said elves didn't do that lightly. I felt like jumping to my feet and doing a touchdown dance. Instead, I smiled. "When you get the first shifter on a Council seat, I'll declare myself your ally."

"Do you have a preference as to whom?"

"I know exactly three shifter leaders. Terra's only been Queen a short time, and she's young." She was also busy, what with making changes to the clan rules, living on her own—well, as much as she could—and of course, having a live-in sweetie. Which left me with one name. I hoped O'Meara would go for the idea. "Nick's dad is a jerk. How about the Rex?"

"I believe he's a good choice."

It occurred to me that Thorandryll might be playing a deep game, because his about-face was truly unexpected. Pretending to be ready to get with the times, and using honey instead of vinegar to get what he wanted. That would be sneaky as hell, therefore, right up his alley.

Then again, if every species did get a Council seat, let him play his game. I glanced at Kethyrdryll, who was smiling at his brother. Or maybe he'd been busy, and after having been assumed dead, was working Thorandryll's relief and joy at his return to the max.

Whichever it proved to be, I would deal with it. "Then when the Rex is on the Council, I'm your ally. Is it okay if I mention it to him?"

"Please do. I don't think he'll take my word without the confirmation of someone he trusts."

"Yeah, being snooty and homicidal toward shifters does tend to make them a teensy bit leery of you." I earned a brief, reproving frown from Kethyrdryll for that. Didn't intend to apologize.

"Now, to mark the occasion of our agreeing to work together, I'd like to offer you a gift." Thorandryll lifted his hands before dropping them to his desk top. "What would you have of me, Miss Jones?"

I hesitated, feeling my eyes narrow. Was this a trick? A way to get me into his debt? But he'd said "gift." "Like what?"

"What do you desire?"

Logan. I managed to keep from grinning, but there it was: I had what I desired. "I can ask for anything, and you'll let me have it, no strings attached?"

"Yes." He smiled, but there was a worried edge to it.

"You're kind of taking a big chance there, dude. What if," I looked around. "I wanted your sidhe?"

Thorandryll's face lost some color. "Is that what you desire?"

"Nah, just wondering." What could I ask him for? I dropped my eyes and picked more pine needles off my coat and jeans. The royal twins stayed silent, letting me think. I wondered what time it was.

Nothing was coming to mind. I wouldn't mind not having a mortgage, but if someone else paid it off, it wouldn't be my house any more. It would, but not really. The clan was happy, so I couldn't think of anything to ask for them.

Oh, but wait. I let the idea solidify before looking up with a smile. "I know exactly what gift I'd like, and it'd be good press for a guy who's running for mayor."

Thorandryll relaxed. "And that is?"

"Two of the biggest issues in Santo Trueno are the homeless, and stray animals. My mom does a lot of charity work for the homeless. The city shelter puts down hundreds of dogs and cats every month." I crossed my legs and bounced the top one. "You guys are really good with animals, and space isn't a problem for you."

"No, it's not." Thorandryll turned his head. "Keth, would you..."

"I'd be delighted to take charge of the animal situation."

The prince smiled, looking at me. "And I'll be honored to offer your mother all of the assistance I can."

I clapped my hands together. "I may even vote for you now."

TWENTY-TWO

"I'm sorry, what did you just say?" Logan was sitting on my bed, watching my attempts to pick out a dress and shoes.

"Shifters are going to be on the Council, starting with O'Meara." Semi-formal. I scanned the handful of dresses in my closet and sighed. "I don't have anything to wear."

He was in black dress slacks, a white shirt, and navy blue suit jacket. "I'm not quite getting from A to B on my own here, Cordi. You said Celadine was there?"

"At first." I had been rushing during my first attempt at explaining. Hm, I couldn't wear the gown I'd gotten for Thorandryll's ball. Not my black and green mini-dress either. "Is showing skin at a vamp party considered an open invitation to being bitten?"

"I doubt it. How does Celadine tie in with shifters getting Council seats?"

Little black dress it was. Mine was a simple, knee-length, sleeveless sheath style. "Oh, she was bitching about getting the mirror back without the spirit."

"Okay, what happened with that?"

I gave him a more complete account while slipping into the dress, and deciding on my black heels. "And then I said 'Newsflash: I'm not your bitch.'"

Logan was laughing. "How'd he take that?"

"He was speechless. Kethyrdryll gave me a standing ovation." I left the closet and posed. "How's this?"

"You're gorgeous."

I preened for a second. "Needs some jewelry. Anyway, we had a talk, and I told him I wouldn't consider being his ally until he started treating everyone with common courtesy. Then he blew me out of the water with putting the leaders, or elected reps, of each species on the Council."

I chose a long, sparkly necklace of crystals in varying size—Christmas present from Mom—and diamond studs. "I hope it's okay I suggested O'Meara."

Logan blinked. "Wait. You picked who'd be first?"

"Well, I told him I'd declare myself his ally when he put the first shifter on a Council seat." I fluffed my hair, using the mirror over my dresser. "Thorandryll asked if I had a preference, and since I only know three shifter leaders, I picked the Rex."

"Why him?" Logan stood. He didn't seem upset, just curious.

"Nick's dad is a pompous ass. Terra's still settling into being Queen. You told me the Rex was tough, but fair." I shrugged, checking my teeth for lipstick. There weren't any smudges. "And I like him, so I picked him."

"Good decision."

I smiled in the dresser mirror. "Thank you."

"We're going to be late."

"Ooh." I dashed back into the closet, and came out with a purple gift bag. "Almost forgot."

Logan raised his eyebrows. "Who is that for?"

"Tase. Look," I showed him the bag's contents. "What do you think?"

"I bet he'll love them."

Logan drove to the Barrows, and we walked to Derrick's. Once there, a liveried attendant guided us from the front door to the end of the great hall. There, tall glass doors stood open, allowing us to hear the soft strains of some instrumental piece. He paused at the door, gesturing for us to step through. "Lady Discordia Jones and Mr. Logan Sayer, Protector of the White Queen."

The announcement of our arrival swiveled heads. I whispered, "Ain't we fancy?"

Logan chuckled, patting my hand, which was tucked over his forearm. We walked down three steps, and I looked around the room. It was an indoor garden, with one large seating group in the center, and smaller ones scattered about, among nooks surrounded by trees and other plants. Conservatory? I thought that might be the correct term.

Aside from not being vampires, we fit in. The women wore simple cocktail dresses, and most of the men were in suits. A few wore dressy shirts and breeches tucked into heavily polished boots.

Derrick met us within a few feet of the steps. "I'm pleased you were able to come. Here." He collected a couple glasses of champagne from a hovering servant, and handed them to us. "Come, let me introduce you around."

"Thank you." I noticed there were a few humans circulating, dressed in black pants and sleeveless, snug-fitting maroon vests. The one closest to us had fresh fang marks on her forearm. She was smiling, and seemed cheerful, so I kept my mouth shut.

Our host followed my line of sight and smiled. "Willing volunteers, I assure you. I don't coerce my donors into serving my guests."

"I didn't say anything."

"And I appreciate your restraint."

The next hour was spent meeting the few dozen vamps in between cooing over rare plants. Logan impressed me with his ability to carry on a conversation about rare plants such as *Lignum vitae* and *Guaiacum santum*, or Tree of Life and Holywood.

All of the vamps behaved like nice, normal people, if I discounted the tendency for odd turns of phrase, some weird slang, and the somewhat stilted formality. Probably because we were there, those who partook of the living refreshments did so discreetly.

It did become slightly uncomfortable once we sat, and along with Stone, were served a small array of finger foods. The other guests gathered around and watched. They weren't exactly staring, just... paying definite attention while continuing their conversations.

Derrick quietly tut-tutted, and that appeared to embarrass those who were more obvious about watching us eat. "Being unable to enjoy solid food has resulted in a certain fascination with watching others enjoy it."

"Oh." For a few seconds, I toyed with the idea of putting on a show for them. Making a big production of nibbling, and maybe do a bit of moaning. Throw in a faux O face or two.

My thoughts of mischief must've been all over my face, because Logan pressed his leg to mine. His tiny smile creases were showing at the corners of his eyes. "Whatever you're planning, please don't."

"Darn." Thwarted, I smiled and reached for another caviar-laden cracker. Our host certainly hadn't stinted on the quality goodies for the three of us. I noticed the volunteer donors had gone, and wondered if they were being fed elsewhere.

Was there a point to this party? I could ask, but the congenial atmosphere made it more fun to speculate. It could be Derrick's idea of desensitization, but whether it was intended for his friends or me, I had no clue. Maybe he just wanted all of us to meet.

Around nine o'clock, the soirée began breaking up. I'd had three glasses of champagne, far too much caviar, and was feeling pretty darn warm and fuzzy inside. I even remembered a few names without prompting, as some of the guests took their leave before we did.

Derrick walked us to the front door. "I do hope you enjoyed yourselves this evening. It was a pleasure to have you both here."

"I never thought I'd have fun hanging out with vampires. But it was fun. Thank you." I let Logan help me into my tiger coat. "I've thought about asking you for dinner, but the menu planning sort of stumped me."

"I'd provide my own nourishment. Bottled, of course."

A giggle escaped me when he winked, and I gave him a thumbs up. "I'll let you know."

"Wonderful."

We made our good-byes and outside, I hugged Logan's arm. "That was way more fun than Thorandryll's ball."

"It was." He kissed the tip of my nose when I tilted my head back. "Thank you."

"For what?"

"Not doing whatever it was that had you grinning earlier, when you were thinking about doing it. Which was what?"

I laughed. "Have you seen *When Harry Met Sally*?"

"Oh, I'm so glad you didn't do that. They'd have lined up to try and steal you away." He grinned. "But it would've been hilarious."

Tase was on the lookout for us, sitting between the front legs of one of the gate's parrot-beaked guards. Upon spotting us, he launched himself airborne with a gleeful squeal, but politely landed on my forearm when I held it up. "Hi! I hoped you'd come to see me tonight."

"And here we are. Hello." I showed him the gift bag. "We brought you a present."

There I went with the cutesy couple thing again. Logan didn't seem to mind.

"You did?" Tase's spade-tipped tail flicked straight out behind him, and quivered.

"Yup. You can open it once we sit down." It took a couple minutes to walk to the table and benches. Tase spread his tiny wings for balance, stroking my coat sleeve and remarking upon its softness.

I felt pleased as heck when the tiny fella dove into the bag, and dragged his gifts out with exclamations of delight. There were two: a soft, floppy, foot-tall brown teddy bear, and a much smaller, green one.

"One to snuggle, one to be snuggled by."

Sitting on the bigger teddy, Tase hugged the green one. It was the smallest teddy bear I could find, about two inches tall. "Thank you. I will take good care of them."

A click turned our attention to Logan, who lowered his phone. "Sorry. The cuteness overwhelmed me. I'll send you the pic."

"What's a pic?" Tase was excited as Logan showed him the picture. "That's me!"

There was nothing for it then, we had to do an impromptu photo shoot. Logan obliged, snapping away, as the baby gargoyle and I posed, made funny faces at each other, and enjoyed acting silly together.

Eventually, we settled down. Tase clutched the green bear, using the bigger one as a couch, and gravely informed me that his lessons were going well. "I made my first charm."

"You did? That's great." I ignored the click from the other side of the table. Logan was obviously stuck in photographer mode. "What's it for?"

"Good luck." Tase lowered his head, and shyly peeked up at me. "I made it for you. I'll go get it."

"Okay." I watched him fly off, and Logan leaned across the table. "I think he may have a crush on you."

"It's mutual. He's just about the most adorable thing I've ever seen."

He fluffed the bigger teddy bear's middle. "He is."

I looked at the sky, and realized there was a full moon. "The moon here doesn't affect you?"

"No, only the true moon does. Which reminds me, I'll be busy on the night of the 22nd."

"Does that mean that pocket realms are kind of like holograms?"

"The skies basically are, if they're not set to Earth normal like ours is."

Tase reappeared, carrying a bright green, small cloth square. "Here it is."

I took the material, and saw that it was actually a bag. The contents felt a bit lumpy, and it was sewn shut, so I couldn't peek at them. "May I ask what's in it?"

He sat up, folding his bitty paws together, and began to recite the ingredients. "There's a tiger's eye, ginseng, vetivert, a bayberry leaf, and dried bluebell."

"You missed one," Logan told him, and the gargoyle wrinkled up his face. "Catnip."

"Oh." Tase nodded. "And catnip."

A good luck charm that was on the cat-centric side. "Well, thank you. I'll keep it with me all the time."

"What else have you learned?" Logan asked him.

Tase moved until he could see both of us, holding his folded paw pose. "Mama's teaching me about all the different things that can be used in charms, potions, and spells. Blood is the most powerful, tears are second, while hair and skin are third. Mama says other bodily fluids don't work very well."

I made a note to start asking for ingredients before I drank any more potions or remedies. "Why is that?"

"They don't work well because they're tainted by food and drink ingestion. Or because of the contamination," he carefully sounded that word out. "In the air. She says that's why no one has to worry about mucus, vomit, or their potty."

"What about nail clippings?"

He rubbed his nose. "Those can be used, like skin."

I nodded, but had to ask, "Wouldn't tears be contaminated or tainted as well?"

Tase shook his head, his tiny mane fluttering. "Tears are different. They're liquid emotion."

My new thing learned for the day. "What can they be used for?"

"Good or ill. Mama says if you put happy tears in a tonic, it will lift the spirits of the one who drinks it."

I wondered how often tears were used, because how easy was it to collect them? What did you do, walk up to someone who was bawling, hold a jar under their eyes, and ask them what they were feeling? "That's fascinating. You're learning a lot."

Tase puffed out his chest, wrinkling his wee snout into a grin. "I am a sponge."

"You certainly are." I bent and kissed the top of his head.

TWENTY-THREE

"The dreaded end of the date is looming." Logan tapped the horn at the driver in front of us, who was weaving a bit. "Or is it?"

"I don't know. This hand," I held up my left hand and pretended it was a puppet. "Says we should keep going. But this one," I lifted my right. "Says we've been getting to bed late a lot, and should get some sleep."

"What do they say to an offer of snuggling, and being, or having, an overnight guest?"

"Hm." I turned both hands to face me, pretended they were talking. "Well, Lefty reminded me that our pack is at your house. Righty just keeps repeating one word: bed."

Logan was grinning. "What if I drop you and your hands off at your house, go pick up the dogs and an overnight bag?"

"What do you say, guys?" I made my hands nod. "They say yes."

"Great."

I turned Lefty to look at him, and tried to mimic my dad's voice. "No hanky panky, Mr. Sayer."

"Yes, sir, Mr. Lefty."

I dropped my hands. "That's okay, right?"

Logan smiled. "Of course it is."

"I don't want you to think," I halted, unable to find the right words.

"I don't think anything except you're tired. Righty said so."

"Okay." The new relationship factor was in full effect. I wanted to spend every possible second with him, but I had done that with my first two boyfriends. Both times had ended with me as a sleep-deprived, over-emotional, rattle-brained mess.

We already spent a lot of time together, and it was far too early to consider asking him to move in. *Whoa, did I just think that?* I really was a goner.

"You're smiling."

"I am." Because I was happy, in love, beginning to live up to my responsibilities, and had finally taken charge of my life.

And it was going way better than I'd ever hoped it might.

Unfortunately, an early bed time and falling asleep quickly didn't make for a restful night. My dreams were chaotic and dark. Then my psychometry visions of the crimes came back to haunt me in full color, holding me frozen as a witness to Mr. Pettigrew's horrible death.

I woke up screaming and crying, disturbing Logan's sleep. He calmed and cuddled me, purring softly, until I fell back to sleep. Another nightmare filled in the time between then and morning. I had to find a gold ball. People were trying to kill me to keep me from being successful. I had to fight and kill them first, because it was important that I find the ball before they did.

I didn't find the damn ball before I woke, and felt snappish and sullen until I'd downed a couple cups of coffee. Logan let me be, taking the dogs out for their morning constitutional, and feeding them breakfast.

He poured himself a cup of coffee once they were crunching away. "Feeling any better yet?"

"Yeah. Sorry for waking you up and being so bitchy this morning." I felt like crap, and had the feeling I looked like it too.

"You didn't sleep well. I can be a huge grump when I don't sleep well, too." Logan went to the fridge. "Doesn't look like I'll be getting another cooking lesson here this morning. Pretty bare in there."

Not feeling up to a grocery shopping trip, I suggested we go out for breakfast. Leglin, sensing my unsettled mood, volunteered to take his pack members to doggy daycare, and I agreed. "That would be a big help. Thanks."

"You're welcome." He wagged his tail when I hugged him. I hugged all of them before the hound gathered them together and poofed away.

As we were headed out the door, Logan asked, "Do you want to drive today?"

"Yeah, I do." I hadn't gotten my beloved chariot out in a few days. Between the doggy hugs, his understanding, and being behind the wheel, my mood rose.

Damian called as we finished breakfast. "There was another break-in last night. A bank, and they didn't follow their usual modus operandi."

"How so?" I pushed Logan's debit card back to him, and put mine with the bill, mouthing "my treat." He nodded, and traded the card for a five, placing it under my card.

"They killed a rent-a-cop, and broke into the vault, but it doesn't appear telekinesis was used for the vault's door."

I smiled at our waitress as she took the payment. "Are you sure?"

"It was opened, but not damaged."

"You know, I can pick simple locks with my TK."

Damian sighed. "I really wish you wouldn't share that kind of thing. I am with the police, you know."

"Yeah, yeah. What I'm saying is, if I can do that, surely someone with a few hundred years or whatever of experience can manage to break into a bank vault."

"Right, but why bother? Why change what was working?"

"Don't know. But I do want to know why didn't you call us last night?" I accepted my card and signed the receipt.

"Because," he drew the word out, "we've reached the limit of how much help you can give us. The perps don't touch anything. That only leaves the remains or personal effects of the victims for you to touch, and so far, that hasn't resulted in images of the perpetrators. Oh, and you tend to bleed, blister, and occasionally, fly into walls when you touch those things. If that's not unsettling enough, the screaming is."

"Sorry." I sighed. "Want us to come in?"

"Go ahead. You can look at the photos. Maybe you or Logan will see something we haven't."

"Okay, we're on our way." I ended the call, dropped my phone into my coat pocket, and put my card away. A flash of bright green inside my purse caught my eye. I pulled out the good luck charm Tase had given me, and transferred it to the pocket of my jeans.

Logan watched and asked, "Think that'll help?"

"Don't know, but it certainly can't hurt." We left the restaurant hand in hand.

"See?" Damian spread out the photos of the vault's door. "Not a scratch on it. Do you really think one of them was able to use TK to unlock it?"

I studied the photos, and shrugged. "Looks kind of complicated to me. I couldn't pick it open."

"One of them could be a master thief," Dane suggested. He'd met us in the parking lot, having driven Logan's truck. He was feeling mopey, but I didn't blame him. At least he was making the effort to take his mind off his breakup.

"Sure, what else do vamps spend their time doing?" Dodson snorted.

I frowned at the photos. "They didn't have electronic locks back in the day. Have there been a lot of night-time bank robberies? He'd have to practice."

"Jones, we haven't had a bank robbery in Santo Trueno since Prohibition." Schumacher wagged his finger at us. "And no, I wasn't on the force then."

I'd had to practice for months before my ability to unlock doors and padlocks had gained any kind of reliability. I still couldn't manage combination locks. A frown took hold, and I looked the photos over again. Something began to wiggle in my brain, practically begging me to pay attention to it.

"The Thieves' Stick," I said, my thoughts a confused jumble. One rose to the top, something Sal had recently said: What appears obvious isn't always the truth.

My thoughts fell abruptly into place.

The stick hadn't worked for Tanisha and her co-workers. Neither had the boots. They didn't have the code word for either. It would take psychometry to discover the code words to use them.

And not only was psychometry an ability vampires didn't have, we knew magical objects rarely worked for them. I looked up, feeling the blood drain from my face. "We're wrong."

"About?" Dodson asked.

"It's not vampires. That's why the guys haven't smelled vampires at any of the scenes. They're not vampires." I was shaking. "The killers are psychics."

He glared. "You said psychics haven't had enough..."

"That's what everyone says about us. Humans who received any magic, I mean. We're behind the learning curve." I gestured at the photos. "And we've believed it. But these psychics aren't, and they've proven it."

Dodson's glare faded. He swallowed. "Then we're in deep shit."

"The deepest."

"You're saying we have a trio of homicidal psychic maniacs running rampage?" Schumacher groaned when I nodded. "I'm too old for this crap."

"It gets worse, because now I'm not certain there's only three of them." I went to the whiteboard and began to write: Telekinesis, teleportation, pyrokinesis, aerokinesis, psychometry, water calling, and light-bending.

Then I added a second list: Telepathy, retro-cognition, and psychic tracking. Stepping back, I capped the dry erase marker. "Ten abilities. Most human psychics, hell, even most vampires don't get more than one or two abilities. Three is rare."

"While you're the psychic unicorn." Damian frowned at the board. "Why did you add those last three?"

"We haven't figured out how they're picking their targets. The museum is easy, because the Fairy Tales display was publicized. But the others?" I pointed at the shorter list. "Those abilities could be the explanation."

"The odds would be high against three psychics with these abilities finding each other, and all be criminally inclined," Stone said.

"Only the three abilities part." Damian kept frowning at the board. "It's not against the odds for the criminally inclined to gravitate to each other. That happens all the damn time."

"Easy part's over then. Now for the hard part. How the hell do we find them?" Schumacher looked around. "Any ideas?"

Dodson stood. "Yeah. It's time we call in the Feds."

The Feds arrived the next day, Friday the eleventh, and took over the case, but agreed to allow us to continue participating to a limited degree. Limited enough that we weren't needed over the weekend.

Nick had been correct. The government had a list of humans who'd become supes during the Melding. I suspected they also had lists of known supes who'd appeared. Nick had mentioned his pack being checked out by doctors. Logan and Terra verified the same had happened with both their clan and their birth clan.

However, keeping tabs on all those supes was a different matter. The government didn't have the necessary manpower for that job. Some were easy to keep track of, like myself. We didn't travel. Some had gone into public service, like Damian. Others were minor celebrities: dog whisperers, or folks with psychometry who verified the provenances of artwork.

And every one of them had to be checked off the list, in order to find out who wasn't where they were supposed to be. Not a simple matter, but one that could take weeks. Maybe even months, because the agents weren't exactly forthcoming about how long that list was.

Meanwhile, the killers continued their spree, hitting a new target that very night.

TWENTY-FOUR

Saturday, I was finally able to look at "my meadow," as Logan kept calling it. We left the dogs with an unshaven, haggard Dane.

"Maybe we should find some happy tears and ask Moira to make him a tonic." I turned in a full circle, surveying the extent of the open area. "Two acres may be too much space."

"He'll work it out. You have to give him some time." Logan spread his arms. "Walling in the whole of it will give you a spot to work on your range without harming or bothering people."

"Okay. How long before it's ready, and how can I help get it that way?"

Dropping his arms, he grinned. "It'll be ready tomorrow. The realm will build it, once we give it the idea to run with."

I was never going to grow accustomed to other kinds of magic. Mine made sense. At least, as much sense as being one of the people able to use a particular form of energy could make. Or maybe, it was familiar enough that it felt like it made sense to me.

But being able to create a magical AI? Mix herbs and stuff together to make people change shapes? Nope. Never would understand that, because how could someone's intentions make those kind of things work?

"How do we do that?"

"First, we should take care of hooking you into the realm. You need to be able to access the AI."

My hands went to my hips, and I tilted my head. "Does thinking of it like it's a computer keep your brain from hurting?"

He laughed. "Yeah, it actually does. Come on, we have to go to the cave behind Moira's."

We joined hands as we began to walk. Logan took the opportunity to explain. "If you think of a pocket realm as a game simulation, it makes all the weird easier to digest. Realms are aware, and that awareness is the AI. People who are hooked in, or blood bound, to a realm can talk to the AI, change the game's settings."

I nodded. "That does make it a lot easier to understand. Is everyone in the clan bound to the realm?"

"Yes. There are safeguards in place, so that no one redecorates the whole thing because of a nightmare or whatever. But everyone can change their houses to suit them, things like that. And like I said, if we were ever invaded, any of us can change our surroundings to hide, or whatever's necessary."

"Do you think that'll ever happen?" I squeezed his hand.

"I hope not. It wouldn't be easy for someone to come in here without permission, but it's not totally impossible either." He glanced at me.

"Yeah, the bad guys got into Thorandryll's pretty easy." I licked the corner of my lips, wishing we'd brought some water. "What about wards? Do we have any here?"

Logan grinned. "That's actually a pretty cool part of things. The only thing that has to be warded is the entrance. The wards—yes, we do have some, hired Ronnie for that job—will sound an alarm if the entrance is bypassed in any fashion."

"I've teleported into here."

"You have a free pass, and no, I don't have our realm letting me secretly know when you pop in." Logan released my hand to give me a boost onto a fallen log. "You're clan. But the AI still tracks all entries and exits people make."

Aha, so that was how the vampire council tracked people. Stone had fibbed a little, about them not keeping as close track of people leaving. Or had he? The Barrows was a mishmash of pocket realms. Maybe that many shoved together didn't work as well as a single one.

He stepped up beside me, and we hopped down together. "If you'll also think of the realm and its AI as a form of internet, then the blood binding creates a wireless connection."

I hadn't thought learning about pocket realms should be at the top of my list, but now that Logan was explaining it, it was fascinating as heck. "How far does that connection reach?"

Logan waved away a fly. "It's capable of alerting us to security breaches or major malfunctions wherever we are. Other than those, we have to be inside the realm to receive messages from the AI."

"That is cool." Blood really was a powerful thing. I needed to be super careful about leaving any lying around.

We continued on, reaching Moira's cabin several minutes later. She was outside, tying herbs in bundles for drying. "Well, hello."

"Hi." I waved, my other hand in Logan's again. She smiled, dusting her hands off on her jeans.

"You two look happy. Things are going well?"

"They are," Logan replied. "We dropped by to let you know we'll be in the cave. Have the time to get Cordi hooked in."

"All right." She came to us, and gave each of us a hug. Stepping back, Moira placed one of her hands on each of our cheeks, a warm smile on her face. "I'm happy for you both."

"Thank you." I should've felt uncomfortable, but Logan was correct: the shamaness was a hard person to feel that way around. It didn't hurt that her pleasure in seeing us together, and in accord, was radiating from our skin-to-skin contact.

Maybe one day, I'd be as good a person as she was.

She dropped her hands. "Feel free to take all the time you like."

Okay, that caused a bit of face warming, but I pretended to miss her innuendo. "Thanks."

We left her to return to her task, and walked around her cabin. Logan proved to know exactly where the entrance to the cave was, and we ducked inside. I again wondered whether he'd done any nude soaking with her, and tried to squelch the thought.

At the edge of the pool, Logan produced a pocket knife. "It only takes a few drops. Do you want to do it?"

I wished he had a needle, but held out my hand for the knife. "Yeah, I can."

"You may want to sit down. It can be kind of overwhelming at first contact."

"Okay." I sat down tailor-style, and opened the knife. He sat down, sideways to me, with one leg bent and partially behind my back. "Does it matter which finger?"

"No."

After a deep breath, I ran the pad of my thumb across the blade's edge. Blood welled instantly, and I held it over the water's surface. Logan took his knife, dipping the blade into the water, while drops fell from my thumb.

"That's good."

I pulled my hand back and applied pressure to my thumb. Once my "encouragement" had enough time to close the small cut, I rinsed off both hands in the water. Drying them on my jeans, I asked, "So when does..."

My vision went black, and I jerked away from the water, my back striking Logan's leg. A series of images flew through my mind so quickly, I couldn't make sense of any of them. Logan's hand was on my knee, and he was telling me to relax.

The stream of images paused on one—us sitting in the cave, by the pool—and then faded completely. I blinked, and the water began bubbling. A figure formed, sliding up until it was facing us. "What the hell?"

Logan chuckled. "It's the AI."

The watery figure spoke, its voice rather bubbly too. "Discordia Angel Jones, clan member and queen. Processing."

Just like a computer. I was suddenly grinning. "You could've mentioned this part."

"And ruin the surprise? No way." He rubbed my back.

"Processing complete. How may I serve you, Cordi?" The AI seemed to be looking at me, or at least, I could see my reflection in its huge, clear eyes.

"What do I do?"

"I'll take care of it." Logan stretched his hand out, and the AI laid a tendril of water on it. Solid water, none dripping. After a few seconds, the AI withdrew its tendril and gave a single nod.

"Your request is processed. The change will be made." And with that, the AI lost all cohesion, becoming a column of water that splashed back into the pool.

"Done," he said. His hand was dry.

"It called me Cordi."

"You did ask all of us to do that. It hears people talking."

I frowned. "Does it watch us when..."

Logan laughed, leaning forward to kiss my cheek. "It's not a person, sweetheart, and it doesn't spy on clan."

"Okay." I had floated naked in that pool. AI water had been in my hooha. "I don't think I'll be soaking in here again."

There was plenty of daylight left to take care of grocery shopping and playtime with my pack. Logan received another cooking lesson, dinner this time, and after, we took a nap.

I had to be at the Blue Orb by eleven-thirty, for Tonya's attempt to attract a familiar, and was. My car was the only one present on the street in the cul de sac.

Jo let me in. "She's nervous, but she's started preparing."

"I came bearing many positive thoughts." I'd never gotten to witness this kind of event before. Following her to the back room, I asked, "How exactly does it work?"

"She's drawing the necessary symbols, and will do the usual to raise a circle. She's picked her offerings over the past couple weeks, so will burn them while making her request."

"Then poof! Her familiar appears?"

My friend grinned. "It's more a slow reveal than a poof thing. Trixie took about twenty minutes to solidify."

"Oh." We'd reached the back room, so I didn't have time to ask more questions. Tonya looked up from inscribing a wiggly symbol with chalk on the polished, cement floor. I gave her two thumbs up with a smile. "Get it, girl."

The teen smiled back, and went back to work. We walked over to the seating area, where Damian, Kate, an obviously pregnant Ronnie, and David waited with their familiars. Kyra, Tonya's Husky, was also present, and I sat down on the floor to scratch her neck.

"Having fun with the Feds?" I asked Damian, who grimaced.

"I liked Agent Kneller much better," he said, naming the agent who'd been willing to listen to us, back when I had had my first retro-cognition, about Henry Wilkins. "Pacelli and Talbot are playing things close to the vest."

Kate snorted. Her crimson hair coordinated with her red and gold makeup scheme, and really popped against all the black she was wearing. Black leather, from toes to neck. "They're government goons."

"Yes, I know." His grin was crooked. "None of us has had a peek at their list, and believe me, we've tried."

"Eh, we're all on it, I'm sure." David flapped his hand. "Doesn't matter much. They can't really do anything, now, can they?"

I could think of things they might be able to do, but wasn't going to mention them while we were all focused on positive thinking for Tonya. Plus, they were kind of out there, aside from simply sneaking up and tazering people. Kyra began panting in my face, and I pushed her nose to the side. "Your breath leaves something to be desired, girl."

"*Sorry.*" She politely closed her jaws. I began scratching her behind the ears.

Tonya called David over to check her work not long after that, and he approved. With a smile that stretched from ear to ear, he called us over and began arranging everyone outside the circle permanently etched into the floor. "You too, Cordi, and Kyra, you stand with her. We want all the positive energy we can get tonight."

Once everyone was in place to his satisfaction, David moved to the spot he'd saved for himself. I realized that he and Damian were facing each other across the circle. I was facing Kate, while Ronnie and Jo were opposite each other. Everyone's familiars were with them. I could just reach Kyra's ear, and touched it when she softly whined.

"All right, Tonya." David nodded at her. "Close your circle."

She had a twig of some sort, and walked the circle with it pointed down, mumbling under her breath. When she reached her starting point, a clear half-bubble sprang into place. A few streaks of gold and silver flashed across its surface before fading away.

I concentrated on thinking about nothing but success for her, my fingers gently massaging Kyra's ear. The only sound was Tonya's voice, as she clearly intoned her request before kneeling and bowing her head over a small, white stone bowl. With a single word, she lit the bowl's contents on fire.

Smoke rose and swirled around inside the bubble, changing colors. My quick peek around showed that everyone outside the circle was smiling, and appeared relaxed. That indicated things were going well.

Tonya lifted her head to watch the center of her workspace. I focused there too, holding my breath. What was she going to get?

Several minutes passed. Nothing else was happening. Another check revealed smiles fading, and the witches beginning to look concerned.

I looked back in time to see Tonya's shoulders sag. "It's not working."

Kyra bumped my leg, and I looked down, feeling disappointed for the girl. The Husky looked up, her blue eyes glowing. "Uh, guys?"

I wasn't loud enough, because David told the teen, "It's okay. We'll try again in a month's time. It's not unusual for the first try to fail, and has no bearing on how well..."

"Guys," I said, much louder, while moving my hand away from the Husky, because a soft, blue glow had completely enveloped Kyra.

That got their attention. Tonya turned around, and nearly fell on her butt as her eyes widened. "Kyra?"

Kate let out a loud whistle, Percy echoing it, and everyone began clapping. While Tonya scrambled to her feet and broke the circle, I looked down at the dog.

Kyra grinned, her tongue lolling out, and gave the doggy equivalent of a shrug. *I chose her years ago.*

TWENTY-FIVE

It was Monday morning, and I was in a great mood, considering the turmoil. Logan and I had spent all of Sunday together, and I'd stayed at his place again, after the weekly clan gathering. We were on our way to the station to see if the Feds had shaken anything loose.

Kethyrdryll had called, eager to tell me all about his new undertaking. I'd been shocked when he told me they'd already rescued over two hundred animals. Thorandryll had given him a staff of fifty elves to get the job done.

"It appears it'll take time to find a property," he said. "It seems to be quite important to find the right location."

I'd hooked him up with my realtor, and family friend, Rita. "She's right. One of the reasons adoptions weren't high is the city shelter's location."

"They will be high now, because one of my teams will collect from the shelter daily."

"You are fantastic."

"It's gratifying to have such a worthy task." In a brisker tone, Kethyrdryll said, "You must come by when you're able. I think you'll be pleased."

"I will, first chance I get." After making that promise, we said good-bye. I put my phone away. "He's having fun."

Logan was smiling. "It's the perfect job for a guy who was content to spend eight years of his life alone with his hound and horse. He loves animals."

"Yeah." I glanced at the empty back seat. Dane had begged off work today. He wasn't getting to sit and brood though. Terra had tagged him to help take inventory of the clan store rooms.

"I'm confused."

Logan had my full attention. "About what?"

"The Feds. How exactly do they plan to capture these guys?"

"Good question." The agents were human. "And I don't know. Maybe that's why they haven't completely shut us out."

He glanced at me, waiting for a car to clear the entrance to the station's parking lot. "How do you feel about going up against the killers?"

"The idea scares the holy hell out of me. But if Stone and Derrick are involved, and have any say in the planning, I'll feel a lot better."

"I would, too. You're not a killer. They are."

Did he mean the vamps, or the bad guys? "I've killed vampires, that cultist with the fake elf ears, and Rhaetha."

Busy guiding his car into a parking spot, Logan shook his head. "I didn't say you weren't capable of killing. But how many of those did you plan to kill?"

"Just one." *Ginger.* I bit my lip and looked out the side window.

He shut off the engine, putting his hand on my thigh a half-second later. "You'll mercy kill, or kill for survival. You don't plan to kill, or kill for kicks."

"No." I hadn't even planned to kill Merriven, had in fact expected him to kill me, backup plan or not.

"They'll have nothing to lose." Logan patted my leg. "Cornered animals often fight the hardest."

"Right." I turned my head and managed a smile. "I'll be careful, if I'm part of the plan."

"I'm not going to lie: I'd rather you weren't. But I know you well enough now. You'll be there if at all possible, for Mr. Pettigrew, for Ernie, for Jeharin, and for their other victims." Logan tucked my hair behind my ear. "I don't know how I love that about you, when it's scaring the hell out of me right now."

"My do-gooder nature does throw me into danger on a regular basis."

He nodded. "But it's who you are. You've got the heart of a guardian, always wanting to help and protect."

"Guess so. We'd better go in, see if they've come up with anything."

"Okay." Logan leaned toward me. "May I have a kiss first, my queen?"

Of course he could.

"Why is everyone staring at us?" Because everyone had been, from the moment we had entered the station. I could feel their eyes following us up the stairs.

"Don't know." Logan's shoulders were slightly hunched, and he'd shoved his hands into his jacket pockets. "Not enjoying it."

"Me neither." I looked over the railing, and some people remembered they had jobs to do. Others continued staring. "It's creeping me out."

An explanation came at the landing, where Stannett stood brandishing a copy of the *Santo Trueno Daily*. "My condolences. You're famous."

"Oh, no." I grabbed the paper, unfolding it to reveal "Psychic Discord Jones: Santo Trueno PD's secret weapon in the fight against crime", and a full-color photo of me jogging with my dogs. A smaller photo of me on Thorandryll's arm was halfway down the front page.

I began cussing a blue streak. Stannett stepped back, his tired blue eyes growing wider with each new word. Damian came out into the hallway, followed by Schumacher and Dodson. By the time I ran out of steam, and let fly a final F-bomb the hall was full of more staring people.

Schumacher began clapping. I blushed as others joined in. "Damn, Jones. Didn't know you had that in you."

"Now you do." I needed to read the article, see how bad the damage was. No telling who the slimy son of a bitch had named, or what the results would be for them. "I need to call my family."

Also, get away from everyone, because I could feel the burn of building tears. Outing me now, while citizens were scared of psychics—damn Brock to hell.

"Use my office," Stannett said.

"Thanks." I hurried to it, keeping my eyes down. Logan followed. He shut the doors and turned, catching me when I threw myself at him. "My life is ruined."

He didn't offer empty platitudes, just held me while I wept. Which I didn't for long because I had an article to read and calls to make.

Twenty minutes later, I flung the paper down, glaring at it. "He freaking named everyone."

"Call your family. I'll start calling the others." Logan rubbed my back. "We'll concentrate on damage control. Okay?"

"Yeah." I swiped at my eyes, a few more angry tears having fallen. "Damage control. I don't know who to call first, Mom or Dad."

"Call Ben." Logan began scrolling through his contact list.

"Because he's the man?"

"No, because he's in advertising." Logan selected a number, hesitating before making his call. "Don't think I didn't catch that jab."

"I'm sorry, that wasn't called for. I'm mad. Shouldn't take it out on you."

"You can, but I'll call you on it. I expect you to do the same for me. Deal?"

"Deal." We both busied ourselves with our phones.

"Hi, honey. Have you seen today's paper?" Dad didn't sound too worried.

"That's why I've called. I..."

"Don't worry about anyone but yourself. The prince called me this morning. He's sent bodyguards." How had Thorandryll gotten my dad's number? Dad kept talking. "So we're fine, your mother included.

Didn't even have to keep the boys home from school. Betty is awestruck."

"She is?"

My dad laughed. "She's the envy of her friends right now."

"Oh." That was unexpected. "The boys?"

"Two elves each. I think archery lessons will be happening after school." Dad's smile came through his voice. "So we're fine, honey. You make sure you are too. Okay?"

"Okay. Love you."

"Love you too. And honey, don't worry about that article. It wasn't bad, considering who wrote it. Good press is invaluable. Bye."

I disconnected and looked at Logan. His call had ended too. "We seem to be late to the party."

"Looks that way. Stone told me 'everything's under control' and to worry about us."

"Thorandryll sent my family bodyguards."

"Nice of him." Logan smiled. "Office or the shop?"

"Office." We made those calls, too, only to be told not to worry, everything was under control.

"The prince advised me he'd see to your family's safety. Has he done so?" Mr. Whitehaven asked.

"Yes, he has."

"Good. Have there been any breakthroughs on the case?"

"Not that I know of." I nodded when Logan gave me a thumbs up. He made another call.

"Don't allow the media attention to distress you. I realize this isn't the best time for it, but aside from the timing and the list of names mentioned, the article's quite complimentary, Discordia."

"Afraid my rose-colored glasses are out of order right now, boss." All I could see were bull's eye targets on my family and friends.

"Would a raise put them in working order?"

Did he just say... "What?"

"We're receiving an alarming number of calls. I believe we're going to be very busy this year."

"Oh." Well, hello bright side. Guess Dad was right. "That's great. I guess."

"We'll discuss it in depth at a later time. Do be careful, my dear."

"You too. Bye." I put my phone away, and caught the tail end of Logan's conversation.

"That'll work. Yes, she's upset." He glanced at me. "But she's doing okay. I'll tell her. Yes, my Queen. Love you too. Bye."

He ended the call. "Terra said don't worry and to remember we have your back. She's sending a few people over to your place, to keep an eye on things."

"That's," my phone rang. Nick's ringtone. I looked at Logan. "Should I answer it?"

"Up to you."

I bit my lip. "Maybe I'd better see what he wants."

Nick had begun talking before I even had the phone to my ear. "...saw the paper. Dad says you and your family are welcome to stay here for as long as necessary. Even your dogs. I really think you should, Cordi."

"I appreciate the offer. Really I do. Please tell your dad I said thank you. But everything is fine. We're all safe. Thorandryll has some of his people watching over my family."

"What about you?"

"I'm surrounded by cops right now. My dogs are safe on clan territory." I didn't get the chance to say anything else.

"We have more people than the tigers. They'll be protecting their Queen." There was a petulant note in Nick's voice. "Not you."

"I'm clan, and I can take care of myself anyway."

"Against other psychics who like blowing up people? I think..."

"Nick."

"What?" he growled.

"Thank you for the offer and for your concern. I'm not going to argue with you. I need to go."

"Are you seeing Thorandryll?"

I sighed. "Good-bye, Nick."

"Cordi..."

I ended the call and adjusted the settings for his contact listing, so his calls would go straight to voicemail. Then I looked at Logan. "He's not going to leave me alone, is he?"

"He loves you. But I will point out he hasn't tried to contact you until now. Unless he has?"

I shook my head. "Last time I talked to him was at Dreamland. He was at Thorandryll's ball, but our paths didn't cross there."

Logan put away his phone. "Then he's been trying to respect your wishes. He's worried about you. If he starts pushing, do what you need to do."

"Right." I'd worry about it later. "Let's go."

"That guy, and that girl." The uniformed cop pointed at the monitor. "I saw both at the first scene."

"Thank you, Officer. That will be all." Agent Pacelli minimized the window before I could sneak a look. He closed his laptop, too. "We'll begin checking street cam footage."

"What do you want us to do?"

"You've been quite helpful, Miss Jones, but I believe we can take it from here. We won't require Mr. Sayer or Mr. Stone any longer either."

He was shutting us out. I didn't move. Agent Pacelli's smile dropped a watt. "Thank you for your aid in this matter. You'll need to clear the room now."

"I'll leave in a minute. Do you have any supes on your team? Because you're going to need them when you find those two and their friends."

"That's not your concern, Jones."

Boy, was he wrong. "Of course it is. I don't want anyone else to die. Not you, not any of your men."

"Your concern is appreciated, but we are trained to handle a variety of situations."

"I know, but seriously, how many times have you guys had to deal with psychics? Believe me, it isn't easy to take on someone who can slide into your head. I've been there, and came damn close to dying."

Agent Pacelli was quiet, studying my face. I tried a little harder. "Please, let us help."

"Your suggestion is appreciated. I'll let you know if we require further assistance." He nodded to someone behind me. "Now, if you'd clear the room, please?"

"Okay." I turned and looked at the agent reaching for my arm. He backed off. "Good luck, dude."

We cleared the room.

TWENTY-SIX

"Could you fake a vision? Pretend to see them dying?" Damian kept his voice low. We had congregated in Stannett's office, which wasn't exactly large enough for seven people.

"Sure, but I wouldn't be able to give particulars. Pacelli would know I had lied once he finds them." I'd gotten a chair, having been right behind Stannett when we'd come in.

"What if someone is able to get the suspect photos for you?" We all looked at Dodson, and he smiled. "We can ask Officer Fuentes what their names are, and look them up."

Stannett partially vetoed the idea. "We can't use the computer system here. It's the Feds' baby now, and we don't want proof we're butting in."

"We don't need to use computers. If Fuentes will let me, I can look at his memories of them." I tapped my leg. "As long as he doesn't tell them, I can say I had a retro-cog."

"I'll go find Fuentes." Schumacher squeezed out of the office.

"The question is, how do we help without stepping on federal toes?" Logan's hands were resting on my shoulders. "I don't think any of us will do well in prison."

I patted his hand. "I wouldn't let any of you guys rot in prison."

Stannett grunted. "No. I think it's best to pass the buck."

He held up his hand when we began protesting. "They're supes. Who better to catch supes than other supes?"

"My master?" Stone asked, and received a grim smile in response.

"If you decided to tell him, and he chooses to do something, well..." Stannett shrugged. "My hands are tied, and my people are out of it."

"Does that include us?" I asked.

"You're civilians. I'm not your boss." He leaned forward. "Try not to get caught. I don't give a damn who gets the credit. I just want these bastards stopped. Hear me?"

I nodded. "Loud and clear."

I sat in the front seat of a patrol car, with Officer Fuentes in the driver's seat.

"All you have to do is relax, think only about the suspects, and let me touch your hand."

Fuentes, a handsome Hispanic with a quick smile, nodded. "I can do that. What if the Feds find out though?"

"That's why we're doing it here, away from the station. Don't talk; they'll never know. I'm going to say I had a vision."

"You're going to lie to the FBI to keep me clear." He studied me, his tawny eyes narrowing. "You could end up in a lot of trouble."

"Maybe." I hoped not, but stopping the killers was my top priority.

"You're all right, Jones. Okay." Fuentes took a cleansing breath and closed his eyes. He held up his hand. "Ready."

I pressed my palm to his and opened a link. The memories were sharp and clear. "Thanks."

He lowered his hand. "You're done? I didn't feel anything."

"All done. Matthew Briar and Renee O'Neal."

He nodded. "That's them."

"Gotta go. Thanks again." I left the car, strolling back to Logan's. Stone didn't look comfy in the backseat. Once in, I twisted around. "Is Derrick awake?"

"Yes, and I called. He's waiting." The dhamphyr touched his forehead. "He's making arrangements as we speak. Our people will be out in force tonight."

"Good." I held out my hand, and Stone took hold. "Here."

I could feel Derrick in his son's mind, an icy shadow that collected the transferred memories. Master vamps were connected to those they'd turned. Derrick would see that all of them received the memories. More than that, he'd share them with the other council members. Apparently, the council working together could broadcast a mental APB.

Every vamp citizen in the Barrows would be on the lookout. Smiling, I turned and sighed in satisfaction. "We're going to get them."

Night fell. We were cruising the streets, waiting for news from the vampires combing the city, or from the station, via messages by parrot. Kate had loaned Percy to Damian.

"They'll strike tonight. They have every night." We'd been told they'd hit places Friday, Saturday, and Sunday nights. The body count was rising. I hoped someone would be in a position to keep them from killing again. Our combined efforts would result in zilch without luck playing a part. Someone still needed to be at the right place, at the right time, to spot the suspects.

The Feds were combing through the traffic and security cam footage. Our "cams" were mobile, fast vampires, so we had something of an advantage.

"Open your window. Percy's behind us." Logan dipped his chin at the rearview mirror. I rolled down the window.

Percy landed in my lap, his wings half-folded. He bobbed his head in greeting. "Feds find hideout. Going there."

"Where?"

"Is place in Palisades. Motel." Percy hummed when I stroked his chest with the backs of my fingers. "On 900 block. Weston."

Stone was already calling Derrick. I scratched Percy's neck. "Good job."

"Cordi give treat?"

I gave him a couple of fries left over from our on-the-go dinner. The parrot gulped them down. "I go back."

"Be careful, and thanks." I helped him to the window. With a squawk, Percy bailed out, the wind catching his wings.

"My master is sending people to the motel," Stone reported.

"Do we go?" Logan asked. About to say yes, I hesitated when the dhampyr's phone rang.

"Yes? Where?" Stone listened to the answer. So did my sharp-eared boyfriend.

"Someone's spotted the woman and two unknown men," Logan said. "They're in a car."

"Let's go there. Where ever 'there' is."

He nodded, and changed lanes before Stone was off the phone. "They're under surveillance."

"We're at four now, and have no idea which of them have which abilities." I remembered the giggle I'd heard, after running into the invisible barrier on Thorandryll's grounds. "Oh, crap."

"What?"

"She was there. O'Neal was still at Thorandryll's. She has aerokinesis, and apparently, the same ability to make herself invisible that Merriven did." I slapped the dash. "Damn it. We could've..."

The dhampyr cut me off. "If she was alone, it would appear she has teleportation as well."

"I guess. There were elves all over the place. The gates were locked down." I huffed, frowning. "Or she wasn't alone, and had a teleporting buddy with her."

"My master is contacting Detective Herde. Spotting a fugitive isn't the same as ignoring the orders of federal agents." Stone chuckled. "Fortunately, it was a strong telepath who spotted them. She will say she picked up a passing thought."

Let's hear it for the vampire doing her duty as a good citizen. "Great. She's not going to confront them, is she?"

"Not alone, unless necessary. Others are on the move to join her."

It was over before we arrived. Their target was another bank, but they hadn't gotten any farther than the lobby.

Vampires can move terrifyingly fast. One had gone and swept the security guard out before the pyro killed him. O'Neal and the teleporter got away. The pyro didn't.

"Meet Liam." Damian was bursting with satisfaction. "Not a nice guy. Few aliases, few dead ex-girlfriends, and now this."

Liam was a short, shaven-head man with a teardrop tattoo under one eye. I knew that kind of tatt signified he'd been in prison. His neck was bloody. So was his mouth. A small, thin blonde stood beside him, carefully re-applying lipstick.

"You missed a bit." I touched my face to show her where the tiny smear of blood was on hers.

"Oh, thank you." She pulled a clean tissue from her purse.

"You did well, Eisha," Stone said. "Our master will be pleased."

The blonde dimpled at him. "Should I stay?"

"Detective Herde?" The dhampyr looked to my friend for an answer.

"We'll need a statement, and is he safe without her around?"

Stone smiled. "He's under control. I think you'll find him quite helpful."

"Oh, yes," Eisha purred. "Liam's going to tell you all he can. Aren't you, my pet?"

"Yes." Liam's reply was monotone.

"And he won't be using his pyro ability." Eisha smiled, displaying delicate fangs. "He has no desire to ever hurt anyone again."

She'd neutered the dude. I was impressed, and rather frightened. Yet another display of the power of blood.

"Detective!" Damian hurried off, leaving us alone with the captured man.

I studied his slack face. "Um, it'd be better if he acted normal."

Eisha nodded. "Of course. Liam."

"Yes, mistress?"

"You will assist the police as ordered, and you will refrain from ever again using your ability to create fire. You will confess to all of the murders you've committed."

"Yes, mistress."

Her dimples reappeared. "And you will do so as yourself."

A scowl broke out on Liam's face. "Yes, you rotten, blood-sucking bitch."

"Charming, isn't he?" Eisha fluttered her eyelashes. "You will never tell anyone that you are under my control."

Rage boiled out from him, but he agreed, calling her the one four-lettered word I never used, which rhymed with runt. Eisha merely laughed. I liked her.

Damian returned. "The Feds' plan went sideways. They have men down, and Briar took Agent Pacelli hostage."

The night wasn't over. Lucky us.

The Old Frontier was in need of a good razing. The motel sat on a corner lot, its hot pink and turquoise paint peeling in wide strips. A modest two stories, it had forty rooms, a tiny lobby, and an apartment behind the front counter.

"Top floor, possibly the hallway. We're not sure who else is in there." Agent Talbot held an icepack to the huge goose egg on his forehead, and one of the paramedics on the scene hovered beside him. He'd been slammed into a door frame. "Bottom floor was cleared before we went up. They knew we were coming."

"Of course they did. At least one of them's a telepath." That was the closest I could get to saying "I told you so." Three agents were dead, two unaccounted for. Agent Pacelli was definitely captured, because they'd seen him at a window, his hands up and a shadowy figure at his back.

"O'Neal and her accomplice are probably up there." Stannett had arrived at the same time we did, along with a SWAT team. "Damian's questioning Liam."

"Who?" Agent Talbot winced.

"One of their gang." Stannett half-smiled. "A citizen alerted us to a possible bank robbery. It was O'Neal and two men. Liam didn't get away."

Everyone jumped, except Stone, when Derrick landed next to his son. I recovered. "You can fly? So not fair that you have transvection."

The vampire lord grinned, sweeping his hair back. "It's a useful talent. What's the situation?"

"Wait a damn minute." Agent Talbot began to stand. The paramedic poked him with her finger, and he plopped back down.

"Do not stand," she told him. "You can run your mouth sitting just as easily."

"You had your chance," Stannett said. "Most of your people are out of the game. I'm back in charge, Agent."

"Look here..." Talbot's second attempt to stand was again thwarted by the paramedic.

"Don't make me strap you down."

Stannett walked away. We traded looks and followed, ignoring the agent's demands for us to stay put. Over by the SWAT van, Stannett halted. "If I send my people in there, they're toast. Herde's the only supe on the force."

"There are nine people in the upper story," Derrick said. "And two bodies. Seven are in the hallway, the bodies are at the end, near the stairs. The other pair is in the northwest corner room. Mm, a prostitute with a customer."

We were staring at him. He smiled. "I have a few people... 'scoping out the situation,' I believe the saying is. Fledglings of mine, quite stealthy."

Stannett shook his head. "You and I need to have a long talk after this."

"I'd be delighted to do so." Derrick half-bowed. His smile faded. "The couple has been discovered. They're all going into a room."

"Three hostages." Damian rubbed the back of his neck. "Confined space."

"And they can leave any damn time they want, with a teleporter on hand." Urgency gnawed at me. "Why haven't they?"

"Good question." Logan slid his arms around my waist. "They want something."

"But what?"

That question was answered ten minutes later, when they released the prostitute's customer. He came out with his skinny arms in the air, dressed in nothing but black socks and white boxers. I did a double-take, because I was positive I'd seen him on TV. In fact, during a commercial for a church. "Don't shoot, for the love of God, don't shoot!"

He had a note. Stannett read it. "They want Agent Pacelli's laptop."

"Why?" I asked then face-palmed. "The list?"

"And they want you to bring it." He looked at me.

"Huh?" My attempt to step back only resulted in firmer contact with Logan. His arms tightened around me.

"I don't like the idea of her going up there alone."

"Me neither." But I would, and he knew it.

Stannett began bagging the note. "If she doesn't they'll send the woman out, via a window."

"Good luck with that. Either Derrick or I can catch her."

He tilted his head, looking at me. "On fire."

"Oh." They weren't playing around. Except, they kind of were. "They could get the damn laptop themselves. Why do they want me to bring it to them?"

"No idea, but we have one hour."

That wasn't much time to come up with a plan. "I need to talk to Liam before I go up there."

"I'll send for the laptop."

I shook my head. "I'll get it after I talk to him."

TWENTY-SEVEN

"Briar has TK and he's telepathic. Renee can cloak and do stuff with air." Liam paused. "Yodal's a fire guy like me. Jimmy and Isobel teleport, and Jimmy can see stuff when he touches things."

That covered most of the abilities we'd figured they had. "What about the sixth person?"

Liam scowled. "He's the one that's gonna kill you, you nosy bitch."

Logan smacked him on the back of the head. Damian and Fuentes pretended not to see it.

"What can he do?" I asked.

Shooting Logan a sullen look, Liam answered.

"He's got TK, gets these visions—that's how we know what we're looking for and how to get to it—and he'll liquefy you from the inside out. You ain't gonna look so pretty, once Frank's done with you."

"I can't wait, but I am curious why Frank's so eager to meet me. Do you know why?" To my relief, I sounded normal. Funny, because my stomach was doing flip flops.

"It was that article. Crowing about how you could be the most powerful psychic in America. Frank thinks he is." Liam grinned. "He don't like it when people challenge him, or when they outshine him."

I was going to kick Nate Brock's family jewels so hard the next time we crossed paths, they'd be lodged in his throat for the rest of his life. "Guess we'll find out, won't we? You've been really helpful, Mr. Scumbucket. Thanks."

He tried to spit on me, but I slapped it back in his face with perhaps too hard of a shove of TK. Too hard, because he hit the side of the patrol car. "Oops. Sor... actually, I'm not. Toodles."

We left Officer Fuentes to put him back in the car, and I led the way back to Stannett and Derrick. "Some guy named Frank is the leader. He's the water caller. How do you stop a water caller? I like my insides just the way they are."

"Can you shield?"

I hesitated, and Damian answered. "She has before."

Derrick tilted his head. "But can you?"

"I don't know. It's only happened a few times."

"You haven't been able to duplicate it."

I shook my head. "Nope."

"I see."

"We're about forty minutes away from Burning Woman," Stannett said. "A good plan would be nice."

"It's usually appeared when I'm in mortal danger."

"Yeah, except when Merriven was beating the hell out of you, or during the battle in the Pit, or when the demons were about to cut you open," Logan said.

"One was a private pocket realm. The other two were out of sync. This is my world," I pointed out.

"Okay, then my next question is, do you think it'll appear?" Logan was watching my eyes.

"He says I'm his favorite psychic." I was putting my faith into my theory that Sal was the being behind that shield. "Do you think a mortal could shield against a god?"

"No," Derrick said. "A mortal being cannot stop a god. Not without the help of another god."

"Then it's got to be him. Okay. I'm going to get the laptop." I touched Logan's arm. "I'll be okay."

"You'd better be." He forced a smile. "You owe me cooking lessons."

No one saw me pop into the station. There wasn't anyone at the office that late, either, when I made another quick stop there.

Surprise people, Sal said, and I planned to. I closed my eyes. "Sal, I don't know if you can hear me, but I'm probably going to need a helping hand in a few minutes. It'd be really nice if you could lend one."

I waited, but there wasn't a response. Had I expected one? Not really. I picked up the laptop again, and returned to the motel. "Got it."

Logan's sniff was barely noticeable. He narrowed his eyes, but didn't say anything.

"I have people in place," Derrick said. "They will enter at the first sign you need them."

"Okay, thanks." I took a deep breath, and another after Logan kissed me. "Let them know I'm coming in."

"Wait a minute. Your first priority is yourself and the hostages. If you can get all three of you clear, just do that. Hear me?" Once I nodded, Stannett dialed the number included on the note. "Jones has the laptop. She's on her way in. Yes, alone."

He nodded, and I started my walk into the motel.

When I stepped through the doors, a female voice came from the left. "You're good at following orders."

"Gee, thanks. Where do I go?" I was hugging the laptop, and letting my fear show in my expression.

O'Neal laughed. "Straight up the stairs. I'll be right behind you."

Did she have a weapon? I really hoped not as I crossed the foyer to the stairs. She wasn't silent, but her footsteps were quiet enough to be hard to hear over the rush of blood in my ears.

Sweat was beginning to flow from my underarms, moistening my shirt. I'd be shopping for a new brand of antiperspirant tomorrow, assuming I made it through the night. Ugh, why did I have to think things like that?

Tase's good luck charm was a lump in my jeans pocket. I'd forgotten about putting it there. Maybe it'd give me an edge. A girl could dream, right?

"Room 236," she said, and poked me in the back with something sharp enough to feel through my coat. "Frank's been dying to meet you."

"So I've heard. Liam says hi." That earned me another sharp poke, and I wasn't sure she didn't break skin.

"Open the door."

Someone did, another of the men. He grinned. "Frank, your girlfriend's here."

I stepped into the room enough to let him shut the door. Didn't know if O'Neal followed me or not.

The room was small, maybe an eight by ten rectangle. The only furniture was a saggy bed, nightstand with two drawers, and a small table with one chair. The bathroom was behind the door, the cabinet with sink on the outside of it, next to the small table.

"Fancy," I said, trying to figure out who was who in the dim lighting. Agent Pacelli and the prostitute were sitting under the single window to the left of the bed. They were against the wall, their hands and feet tied together. The hooker was a skinny brunette with tear-smeared, heavy makeup; she couldn't have been more than sixteen. *Holy crap.*

"You're a smart ass." The man who'd spoken was reclining on the sagging bed, his arms and ankles crossed. "I don't like smart asses."

"And I don't like psychopaths, so I guess we're even, huh?" One day, I'd be scared speechless. Today was not that day. I held out the laptop. "Here it is."

Frank was white, well-built, and ugly as sin. A thick scar ran down his jaw and neck. I wondered what had made it. His eyes were too small for his face, while his nose looked like someone had broken it several times, leaving it a shapeless blob. He had buzzed, black hair.

A flicker of shadow at the window caught my attention, but I didn't dare try for a closer look. Just knowing there was a vampire out there, and on my side, helped steady my nerves. I smiled, giving the laptop a wiggle. "You do want this, right?"

The other four were as spread around the room as possible. Isobel sat down on the bed's right side. She was tiny, with a pointy chin and short, wispy brown hair. "Want me to grab her heart for you?"

I felt my eyes narrow, and cocked my head to stare at her. Could she actually teleport a body organ out of someone? What a disgusting idea.

"Take it," Frank ordered, and the man closest to me grabbed the laptop. I let him have it, immediately straightening my coat.

"You got what you wanted. How about letting those two walk out of here?" I jerked my chin at Pacelli and the girl.

"How about you close your mouth, before I close it for you?" The guy who spoke was my height, and built like a brick wall. His arms were bigger around than my thighs. "I'll melt your lips together."

He was the other pyro, Yodal. Check. I had four identified now. Not sure what use that'd be, but it was something. If they decided to jump me all at once, I was dead. Unless Sal had been listening, and jumpstarted a shield for me.

"Back off, Yodal." Frank scratched at his scar, squinting at me. "I'm gonna give you one chance to make the right decision, girly."

"About what?"

"About joining us."

"Oh. Okay, give me the sales pitch." Not what I had expected, after my talk with Liam, but I put on an expression of interest, and gestured at Pacelli, who stared back. There was dried blood down the side of his face from a minor scalp wound. "I mean, it's not like he offered me a job."

"We're the top of the heap. We can break into anything, go anywhere, and no one can stop us." Frank paused. "We can live like kings and queens, taking whatever we want, whenever we want it."

"Right, so why take a bunch of magical junk?" I asked, wondering exactly what I was supposed to do. Too bad I hadn't practiced teleporting stuff I wasn't touching. A cell phone was one thing. Two people? Entirely different.

"Because we can," one of the other men said. "If we have it, they can't use it against us."

"Smart." I kind of needed some guidance, and flicked a glance at Pacelli. He frowned. "If I join you, what do I get? See, I'm already a queen."

Frank smiled. "I didn't say the offer included you being one of us."

There it was, Liam being right. "Well, that sucks. I guess my answer will have to be no then."

He lifted his hand, and my breath caught as I glanced at it. A dark stone winked at me from the ring on one of his fingers. "I think your answer's yes. Isn't it?"

Bastard had cracked the code on Thorandryll's mesmerizing ring. I felt myself nod, my face going slack. Frank moved his hand, and my eyes followed the ring. "I got her. Told you assholes it'd be easy with this."

I was so screwed.

"Make her do something." Isobel crawled onto the bed, and put her hand on his leg. She licked her lips, watching me. "Make her kill the hooker."

The prostitute began to sob and beg. Agent Pacelli closed his eyes.

"That would make it clear who's boss, huh?" Frank nodded. "All right. Jones, throw the hooker out the window."

I didn't try to fight the order, because I knew there was a vampire outside. Just used my TK to lift her, and sent her flying backward. Glass shattered and broke as she screamed, dropping from sight. A blur followed her, and I breathed a private sigh of relief as those in the room began laughing. She wouldn't end up splattered, but I hoped she hadn't been cut too badly, going through.

Agent Pacelli was glaring at me. Let him... as if I could do anything about that anyway. Frank's lowering of his hand didn't matter. I was under the ring's spell, and didn't have to see it anymore.

There had to be something I could do, but at that moment, nothing was coming to mind.

TWENTY-EIGHT

Frank ordered me to stand beside the door and not use any of my abilities. I obeyed, because trying to resist didn't work. The psychic band of psychos were in no hurry to vacate, appearing completely unconcerned by the knowledge that the place was surrounded.

No vampires came bursting in either. I figured that had to mean the one by the window had heard or seen enough for them to realize what had happened.

Logan would be worried sick, and I couldn't contact him to let him know I was all right. Well, mostly all right.

Unless I could break free of the ring's spell, when they decided it was time to leave, I'd be going with them. I'd become a murderer, killing people because Frank wanted me to. I'd probably never see my family or friends again. I'd never see my dogs or Logan again.

The realization sent a tear down my cheek, and Pacelli's glare softened. He was watching me, but listening to them as they fought over which city they were going to rampage through next, and with how much of a bang they'd leave Santo Trueno.

"I say we blow everyone down there sky high," Yodal said.

"Even better, make her do it." Isobel pointed at me. "Bet some of her friends are down there."

"Her guy's down there." It had to be Briar speaking. Liam had said he was the one with telepathy. "Shifter named Logan."

When had he found that out? Had he been eavesdropping on us, or did he pick it out of my mind when I was thinking about Logan a minute ago? Or he could've gotten that information from Pacelli. It wasn't exactly a secret. Nothing was secret, when Schumacher was determined to tease you.

Frank scowled. "That could be a problem. Jimmy, why don't you grab her guy, bring him up here?"

"You want me to drop in on a bunch of armed cops?" Jimmy shook his head. He'd been the one who'd taken the laptop from me. "No way in hell. They got that pretty boy vampire down there. I heard Renee tell you that."

166

Crap, had O'Neal seen the other vamps? I hadn't, and didn't think anyone else had, either. We only knew they were there because Derrick had told us so. I flicked a look at Briar, but he didn't seem to be focused on me.

"I'll go get him." Isobel stood and stretched, before cracking her knuckles. Her thin lips stretched into a leer. "Can we keep him for a while? It'd be fun."

"Get him, and we'll see." Frank twisted the ring around his finger. "Might keep him as a whipping boy for her."

No, no, no. This is not happening. I watched Isobel blink out of existence, my mind spinning.

"Nah, let's just kill him. Nice and slow, while she watches." Yodal called dancing flames to his fingertips. "I haven't had much fun lately."

My fear went up in flames of my own as anger filled me. He had to go down first, Frank second. Those two were the scariest. If O'Neal were outside the room, she'd have to open the door to come in, cloaked or not. How long would it be before Isobel returned with Logan?

Maybe she wouldn't. Derrick and Stone were both out there. Logan was with them.

I heard a faint sound out in the hallway, followed by a thump loud enough to attract Briar's attention. "Something's going on out there."

"Then go check." Frank pointed at me. "You come over here, stand in the corner by me."

My legs felt like lead as I moved. The new vantage point gave me an excellent view of the door, but I could barely see the window, and Pacelli's head, from the corner of my eye. I could've reached out to strangle Frank, if I'd been able to move my arms. I was angry enough to do it.

Briar and Yodal went to check, leaving the door open.

"Think I'll let Yodal have her guy. He's getting on my nerves with his whining, the sick bastard." Frank scratched at his scar again. "I don't like shifters anyway."

"Isobel does." Jimmy was shivering. He was bone thin, and his teeth weren't in great shape. Meth head? "She screwed her way through nearly the whole pack, back home."

"She ain't screwing this guy."

No, she was not. Logan was *mine*. The thought growled through my mind, and I thought another echoed it. She wasn't going to touch him, Yodal wasn't going to torture him.

Jimmy fidgeted, looking at the door. "What's taking them so long?"

"Calm down, and stay put. You're my ticket out of here."

Jimmy didn't move, but he also didn't calm down. "Shouldn't she be back with the guy now?"

Pacelli chuckled. "I think your friends may have run into trouble."

Oh, now he wanted to help. My insides squirmed, and I wondered if Sal had hitched a ride again, but the movement didn't feel the same, exactly.

"Shut up." Frank waved a hand in the agent's direction, and specks of blood broke out on Pacelli's face and hands. "I don't need you anymore."

"What if he's right? Isobel should've been back. The guys have been gone too long. Maybe that sound was someone jumping Renee." Jimmy was scratching his arms, his eyes blinking at a furious rate.

"I am right," Pacelli said. "It's just you two now. They're captured."

"I said, shut up." Frank's second wave brought blood pouring out of the agent, who screamed in shocked pain.

Repulsed, I tried to move, but nothing happened. I couldn't even yell at Frank to stop.

I need help. Sal! My mental scream appeared to go unanswered, but then I realized my right arm was moving. Neither of the men noticed, Jimmy dancing back from Pacelli's bloody, screaming figure, and Frank watching the agent bleed.

The squirming had stopped, but something was still moving inside me, and it had control. My hand dove into my coat, under my shirt, and grabbed.

A second later, I was free of the spell, my ears ringing from the shot. Pacelli fell silent, Jimmy blinked out of sight, and slowly, oh so slowly, Frank toppled over onto his side.

I'd shot him. Or rather, whatever had taken control of my body had shot him.

Isobel reappeared, clinging to Logan's back with her arms around his neck. She sang out, "Got him!"

I swung my gun from Frank's body to her head. "I got someone too. Now it's your turn."

Surprised, she didn't react fast enough. Logan took three steps back, slamming her into the wall. Her head bounced off, and her eyes fluttered shut. Lowering my gun, I said, "We need to get Pacelli to the ambulance."

"Are you okay?" He let her drop to the floor by taking a step forward.

"I'm fine. Pacelli's not." I tucked my gun into my coat pocket, listening to the soft, satisfied purr echoing in my mind.

<hr/>

"You used your gun?" If Damian's eyes grew any wider, his eyeballs were going to fall out of his head.

I dropped it into the baggie Schumacher was holding out. "I do have a license, and I practice."

"Yeah, under duress. Kate's shared how much you complain about that. But you never carry it."

"It's a good thing she did." Pacelli winced. He was on a gurney, already hooked up to an IV. They'd cleaned some of the blood from his face. "He was killing me."

Stannett stood with his arms crossed. "You said you were under the influence of that ring."

"I was. Guess hearing him screaming was the final kicker in breaking free. I'd been fighting it the whole time." I signed the paper Schumacher shoved under my nose, and calmly continued lying. "I didn't know what using TK or whatever on Frank would do. But I figured a bullet would stop him, and what he was doing to Pacelli, for sure."

Damian was shaking his head. "You *never* carry your gun. Why did you even have it?"

"Someone told me I was becoming too predictable." I gave Schumacher his pen back. "I'm trying not to be predictable anymore."

"Is that really what happened?" Logan looked over from the driver's seat.

"Was it that obvious I was lying?"

He chuckled. "No."

"I couldn't break free." I hesitated. "I tried, especially when they were talking about bringing you up and killing you. Or rather, letting Yodal slowly burn you to death. But I couldn't break free of the spell."

Logan nodded. "So how'd you manage to shoot the guy?"

"I didn't. Cerridwen woke up, and she did." There was no other explanation, especially with the purring afterward. "But I think she's back asleep now. Or maybe she's left. I don't know."

"Okay, so the First Queen's spirit woke up, took over your body, and managed to shoot the guy right in the head." He nodded. "Makes perfect sense."

"No it doesn't, but it's what happened." I was tired, and there was blood on my coat from Pacelli. "This is one of those nights when I really wish I was a normal person."

Logan put his hand on my leg. "If you were a normal person, you'd be dead."

Couldn't argue with that.

TWENTY-NINE

The lawn party was in full swing, and there were certainly things to celebrate. We'd stopped the psychotic psychics' reign of terror, Tonya had discovered her familiar, and the Rex, James O'Meara, was now a member of the Council.

Arcane Solutions was booked solid for the next two months, and Mr. Whitehaven was hiring three new investigators to help cover the increased work load. We'd all gotten raises, and I was far less worried about ending up in the poor house.

Brock's article had done more good than harm, at least for now, but I wasn't willing to forgive him for throwing my family and friends to the media wolves. Thorandryll's run for mayor had become national news, and because of the romantic association Brock had implied existed between us, I'd had to change numbers to stop the calls from reporters.

Logan walked up, carrying two tall glasses of iced juice. "Here you go."

"Thanks." I'd found a relatively quiet spot on the edge of the madness. People and dogs were milling all over the place. Kethyrdryll was darting around, smiling, welcoming new arrivals, and making certain everyone was having fun. "He looks happy."

"It's his first official Adoption Day. He told me that twelve dogs have already found their new owners." Logan sat down on the grass beside me. "You, on the other hand, don't look happy."

"Brock's here. I'm trying to keep everyone between us. I don't think I can resist the urge to kick the hell out of him, if we get within ten feet of each other." I took a drink.

"Is that all that's bothering you?"

"No. I'm wondering where Jimmy went." He'd been the only one of Frank's gang who hadn't gotten caught. Possibly didn't matter, since he could only teleport. The way he'd cut and run displayed a certain lack of loyalty. If I'd been right about his drug of choice, Jimmy was well down the path of self-destruction.

"Anything else?" Logan was watching my face. I frowned.

"I'm not sure how I feel about having Cerridwen inside me. It was okay at first, because she helped find you. And I know we both might not be sitting here right now, if not for her taking action. But why is she still here?"

"I don't know, but I feel certain she won't hurt you, if that's what you're worried about." He pushed my hair off my shoulder before kissing it. "You could try asking her to leave."

I had, and there'd been no response. She might already be gone, but I'd had a few dreams that indicated otherwise, because they were too vivid. I'd never hunted for food, unless you counted trying to find an open grocery store late at night.

"Is it because she took over your body?"

I looked at him. "Wouldn't that freak you out?"

"Probably. But she did it to help."

A long sigh escaped me. "I'm just tired of being used. Thorandryll's used me, Sal and Cernunnos used me, Frank used me, demons have tried to use me, and now her, even if it was to help."

Logan nodded. "I can understand that."

"I'm being a total downer. We're supposed to be having fun." I spotted my mom, and waved, pasting a big smile on my face for her. She waved back, hanging onto Edrel's arm. The pale-haired elf had been assigned as one of her body guards, and Mom was taking full advantage of it.

"Then let's look on the bright side. It's a beautiful day, here anyway." We were in Thorandryll's realm. "We're surrounded by people having a great time, happy dogs, and if you haven't already, you should really go check out the buffet."

"I should, huh?" I was feeling a bit peckish.

"Oh, you should." Logan smiled. "I don't even know what half of it is, so could use some help filling a plate."

"Sounds tempting." I learned closer to him. "You forgot the best 'bright side' thing."

"Which is?"

"We're here together." Our lips met, and I let my worries fade away for the moment. Then I recalled how awesome the food at the ball had been. I still needed to figure out how to kidnap Thorandryll's chef. "Okay, let's go check out the food."

We climbed to our feet, and joined the throng of people. I felt the nudge of a cold nose on my elbow and looked. Leglin wagged his tail, knocking one of the servers clean off his feet, and sending another man staggering sideways.

"Oh, gosh." I handed Logan my glass, ignoring the hound-induced chaos that was ensuing, and took the little black and tan puppy from Leglin's mouth. "Oh, you are so cute."

"Cordi." Logan nodded at the ground. I looked down to find another tiny, reddish brown pup huddling between Leglin's front legs. I swooped it up, and snuggled them both under my chin. Puppy kisses soon followed.

"*May we keep them?*" My hound asked, still wagging his tail, while bystanders made sure to steer clear. "*Please?*"
So much for that raise.

About the Author

Puppy rescuer and equine slave who loves visiting other worlds through reading and writing.

If you're interested in news and future releases, you can find her on Facebook (http://www.facebook.com/G.L.Drummond), Twitter (@Scath), or visit her author web site at http://gldrummond.com.

The Discord Jones urban fantasy series has its own web site at http://discordjones.com.

Printed in Great Britain
by Amazon